# about the book

Scoop and Scandal

*They're rival reporters chasing
the biggest scoop Comet Cove has ever seen.
She wants a serious story. He wants glitz and gossip.
The problem is, they just might want each other.*

Comet Cove, Florida, is all about stars. Star Harbor, Stargazer Point, and a galaxy of space-themed businesses draw more and more famous folks escaping their celebrity lives for a stay in this quiet, quirky town. But when a fishing boat explodes in the Atlantic with a beloved actor on board, the big bang shakes up more than the glitterati.

Fueled on mochas from Bean Me Up, reporter Roz Melander rushes to land the biggest story her beach town has seen in years. Who was aboard the boat? And what caused the blast? Solving the mystery could help her save her family's struggling *Courier* and get her back to her big-city career.

But her annoyingly handsome rival, newshound Alden

Knox, is one step ahead of her. A cynical former tabloid scribe, Alden nets scoops for the fluffy *Beacon*, chasing the VIPs flocking to Comet Cove. And with every quip and quibble he throws at her, he gets on Roz's last nerve.

As the story throws them together, they both run to get it first—but when they run into danger, they realize someone will do anything to stop them. Teaming up to foil a dangerous enemy might keep them alive, but now they have another problem. One of them has to win. And given their inconvenient attraction, winning might hurt just as much as losing, especially if their hearts get in the way of their deadlines.

*Scoop and Scandal* is a low-spice funny romantic mystery. This novel contains mild cursing, unabashed longing, closed-door canoodling and lots of giggles.

# SCOOP and SCANDAL

## Comet Cove Mysteries
## Book One

# LUCY LAKESTONE

Velvet Petal Press
*Florida*

*for the ink-stained wretches*

# Map of Comet Cove, Florida

*Fanciful and not to scale*

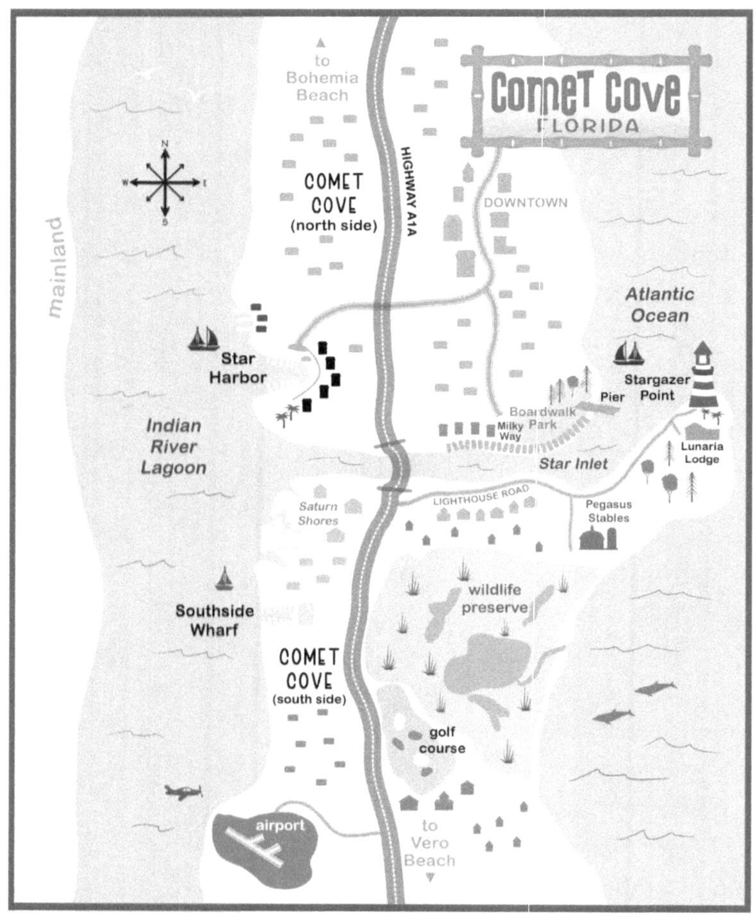

# chapter
## one

*Once upon a time in Florida*

THE RUMBLE SHOOK Roz Melander right to her bones.

"It's too early for a thunderstorm, isn't it?" She looked out the front window of the coffee shop, still feeling the boom. Her nose for news longed to sniff out a story in Comet Cove that might rival what she'd left behind at the Baltimore paper.

"I don't know what that was," said Lily. The skinny blond barista who worked weekday mornings at Bean Me Up tapped Roz's iced mocha order into the register.

Since her return to balmy Florida, Roz craved cold treats, from her coffee to the occasional cone at the Milky Way, where she'd spent many a high school date. Icy goodies were the one vice she allowed herself, the only one she had time for. Well, that and the occasional glass of wine after a long day of work. And they were all long.

"Maybe my brother drove by," Lily added, trying to explain the noise. "His old Charger backfires all the time."

"Maybe," Roz said, handing over the toll for her morning caffeine. But she doubted a bang that big came from a backfire. Besides, it didn't sound like it happened right outside. So where?

She checked her phone. No rocket launch this morning, so no falling boosters and no sonic boom. She tucked her phone back in her bag and took a minute to appreciate the space and UFO art on the walls, sneaking a glance at a pod of old guys who sat in the back of the sunny cafe, solving the world's problems. Plus one Grammy-winning pop diva wearing headphones and hiding behind a laptop. Roz still wasn't used to stumbling over celebrities wherever she went in her old hometown, which had, to her puzzlement, become a star magnet. But she respected their space.

She turned and narrowed her eyes at a new arrival who'd set the door jingling.

The door and her nerves.

She hadn't been properly introduced, but she knew his byline in *The Beacon*: Alden Knox. While Roz struggled to save the staid *Comet Cove Courier*—the newspaper had just cut back from daily to weekly print publication to focus on online news —the newer *Beacon* had more sparkle than substance.

Online and in its colorful weekly, *The Beacon* profiled lavish houses, pretty people and ritzy restaurants. Alden, its chief newshound, chased scoops on celebrities—apt, since it seemed more stars bought homes here every day. Others flocked to a growing number of upscale hotels, including Lunaria Lodge. The new resort sprawled on a scenic point on the Atlantic Ocean by the lighthouse, on the south side of the inlet that split Comet Cove.

Alden nodded at Roz, blinked as he spied the pop star, then flashed his million-dollar smile at Lily. "Morning."

"Your usual?" The clerk paused in brewing Roz's mocha, pushed a lock of hair out of her face and smiled back at Alden.

"As long as it's hot," he purred in that cursedly smooth voice, no mistaking the double entendre.

Roz couldn't get *hot* out of her head as she pretended to ignore him. He had to know how attractive he was, and that made him all the more annoying. He made casual look couture —jeans that clung in all the right places and a white, button-up shirt whose partially rolled sleeves showed off muscular arms and an enviable tan. Under dark, expressive eyebrows, his cool gray eyes took in everything with an almost sleepy disregard. He had a long, straight nose, a strong chin dusted with scruff, and a distracting mouth forever on the verge of a sardonic quirk. His dark brown hair was precision-cut, just long enough to tempt a woman to run her fingers through it—some lonely, needy woman who was an easy mark for that debonair act.

Not her.

Roz had another agenda. One: Save the family business so her ailing mother would have something viable to sell. Two: Cover the news while running circles around this guy. Three: Get back to the city and the investigative team so she could salvage her career.

"Iced mocha!" Lily handed the tall paper cup to Roz and tapped her screen again.

"You're a goddess." Roz cradled the cup and prepared to scoot around her rival.

But then, as Alden stepped closer to the counter and touched his card to the reader, he spoke. "Working on anything interesting?"

It was the first time he'd ever said a word to her. Roz, dumbstruck, met those piercing gray eyes, and her breath hitched.

And then the sirens started.

Alden's perfect right eyebrow shot up at the sound. Roz shrugged, trying to appear nonchalant.

"Maybe I am now," she replied as she pushed out the door.

ALDEN SMILED AGAIN AT LILY, mentally reminded himself to write something about the pop diva, and casually sipped his hot black coffee on his way out into the cool February morning. He didn't want to look as if he were running after his rival.

He'd seen Rosalind Melander, as her byline called her, four or five times a week since he'd moved to Comet Cove a month ago, in January. It took him less than a day to figure out who she was. After all, her *Courier* had only three journalists who did all the reporting, editing and photography. His publication, *The Beacon,* had five, including a dedicated photographer, plus a stable of freelancers. It wasn't hard to discern who was writing what by power of deduction.

And after he saw her, he *needed* to know who she was.

He'd first encountered her at the Meteor Mart, the shop at the gas station a few blocks from Bean Me Up. She was telling Mrs. Yung, the skeptical lady who ran the convenience store, that the *Courier* should be placed above *The Beacon* in the rack.

Alden hadn't been able to take his eyes off Ms. Melander, as he'd come to think of her. There was something about her no-nonsense attitude that precluded the use of first names.

He didn't know if it had been her provocative curves, the captivating bounce of her long, reddish-brown hair or the green flash in her hazel eyes, but something about her stopped him like a red cape whipped in front of a bull. He stuttered to a halt, panting, scuffing the ground with his feet, at least on the inside.

On the outside, he pretended a definite lack of interest and, after she left, charmed the shopkeeper into displaying *The Beacon* on top.

Most women seemed to love Alden whether he showed interest or not. But whenever he was around Ms. Melander, whatever he did, he just seemed to tick her off. She'd never said a word to him until now, but she gave off enough frosty vibes to chill his coffee.

Maybe they *were* rivals, but it was a small town, and it didn't hurt to be friendly, did it? Each time Alden watched her lush pink lips purse in frustration, he longed to be very friendly indeed.

They crossed paths only at the coffee shop or where their divergent beats intersected. A zoning meeting on the expansion of the golf club and championship course? Sure, he'd been there, scrutinizing its fat-cat investors for the kind of celebrity news that did well locally and nationally online. Ms. Melander covered the traffic issues and concerns over whether excessive irrigation and fertilizer would spoil the adjacent wildlife preserve. The council approved the expansion anyway. Dull stuff, really. The kind of stuff he used to cover when he started in journalism, before everything went wrong and he went to work for the tabloids instead.

It was the deep-pocketed owner of his last publication, the *National Eye,* who'd invited Alden to join his hobby project in the community where he was building a mansion. Like Citizen Kane, the publisher thought it might be fun to run a newspaper. He'd be able to inject his opinions and friends into its coverage of Comet Cove, which thrived on a wide spot in the chain of barrier islands that ran along much of Florida's east coast. Thus *The Beacon* was born.

A growing influx of glitterati offered endless fodder for celebrity news that gave them a national audience as well as a local one. Alden, his colleague Kat and a leisure-minded sports reporter wrote mostly harmless, star-studded fluff pieces, a lot less seedy than the items he'd penned for the *National Eye*. But if Alden happened to uncover a few salacious details when reporting one of his gossipy stories, he delivered, and their traffic shot up accordingly.

Another perk: The hours were a lot less horrible than they'd been at the *National Eye*. One of these days, Alden might even write that novel he'd been pondering for years. Maybe it should be about a journalist, he mused. A pretty, stuck-up journalist who was driving him crazy.

Like Bean Me Up, his office at *The Beacon* was on Main Street, a block beyond the *Courier*, and he picked up his pace when he got out of the coffee shop. He didn't see Ms. Melander anywhere, and that was just as well. The sirens probably signified a house fire or a car wreck or something, nothing he'd be interested in covering, unless someone famous was involved. Though there had been that curious noise just as he'd parked at the office.

He'd get back there and listen to the scanner first to see what he could glean before heading out on a wild goose chase. Kat wouldn't come in till the afternoon, because she had a charity wingding to cover tonight, and the sports guy was probably hounding golf pros for quotes. His editor might be around, though.

Downtown Comet Cove was ruthlessly quaint, lined with palms and oaks and filled with shops, restaurants and scrappy little businesses that were getting more upscale all the time:

Aurora's, a clothing boutique. The Orbit, a cool bar. Twinkle Twinkle Toys. Pluto's Pizza. Big Bang Books, known for its science fiction, comic book and romance collections. And the beautiful old Moonlight Theater with its neon crescent moon at the center of the marquee.

Across the street from the theater, the handsome peachy stucco building that held the *Courier* office fit right into the town's Florida style, and he studiously ignored it as he strolled by.

But he couldn't ignore the sound of a car peeling out of its space a moment later and hurtling past him. He knew that car. He had an eye for them. It was Ms. Melander's little silver hybrid, and she was in a hurry.

Alden increased his pace and walked into his much more modern office, where the ad and design staff was busy on the first floor. He trotted up the stairs to the second, which housed the glassed-in office suite of the publisher—absent as usual, though behind the glass, executive assistant Helen stared intently at her computer. Perpendicular to the suite was another office—the smaller fishbowl where the editor worked —as well as a conference room.

The bullpen outside the executive offices held a coffee station, a table for meetings, and a handful of desks for the reporters and photographer, plus some extras the freelancers occasionally used. One of those held the radio scanner, which Alden turned up before he sat at his desk and cranked up his laptop.

Alden's workspace was mildly messy, with piles of magazines and newspapers, notebooks, a foot-high bust of Shakespeare wearing a Bohemia Beach bucket hat, a half-eaten can of cocktail peanuts and one well-hidden volume of seventeenth-century poetry. He took another gulp of coffee and tried to make out what the police were saying on the radio.

John Restyn, his editor, leaned back in his chair in his glass-walled office. One pink cheek bulged with his habitual wad of gum, a legacy of giving up smoking. He frowned as he talked on an old-school landline, the phone receiver wedged between his chin and shoulder. Alden waved at him, but John waved him off, as if he were swatting away a fly. Alden smiled. He liked John, an old-school editor who never stopped longing for the days when news was news.

An unusual note of excitement in the local cop transmissions caught Alden's attention. The deputies didn't have much of a filter, and the small department hadn't yet upgraded to encrypted communications. For both of these things, he was grateful.

He typed key words into a new document as he heard them on the radio: *boat ... smoke ... possible explosion ...* This was getting interesting, even for him. *Coast Guard ... Star Harbor ...* It sounded as if the sheriff's office was deploying a boat to investigate something, and the Coast Guard was already en route.

And then he heard: *This might be one for the coroner ... possible guest at Lunaria Lodge ...*

One thing was almost certain about guests at Lunaria Lodge. They were rich. And sometimes, they were famous. Which meant, for *The Beacon,* they were news.

Alden practically flew down the stairs and out to the street, cursing his dilly-dallying. He ran to his well-seasoned, tomato-red Miata convertible and cranked it up.

"I'll be damned if she gets the story first," he muttered as he shot out of his space and headed for Star Harbor.

# chapter
## two

ROZ ZOOMED into the Star Harbor lot and squeezed her car into a tiny space as close to the boats as she could get. Actually, the space might have been for a motorcycle, but she was press, and sometimes, she just needed to park up front. Besides, there were half a dozen other empty motorcycle spots, which gave her a moment's pause. Did a lot of bikers own boats? Maybe there was a trend story in there somewhere.

A line of colorful waterfront businesses across the street, bristling with gift shops, restaurants and bars that drew tourists and nightlife, ensured parking was always at a premium here. Illustrating the point: Two Comet Cove sheriff's deputies' cars were double-parked near the harbor office, and she knew from what she'd heard on the scanner that the cops were too busy with other things to ticket her.

Star Harbor was the town's biggest marina. Its name grew out of a space theme inspired when city founders incorporated Comet Cove in 1910, naming it for the two renowned comets that dazzled Earth that year. During the moon-shot days in the 1960s, when the space program boomed a few dozen miles north in Cape Canaveral, the town doubled down on its history, so there were a lot of spacey places here.

Just north of Comet Cove was Bohemia Beach. To the south, Vero Beach and Fort Pierce. The barrier islands had few breaks that offered access to the ocean, so Comet Cove's inlet was popular among casual and professional mariners alike.

Star Harbor's home on the northwest side of the inlet, on the usually calm Indian River Lagoon, was perfectly situated to offer access to either body of water. But the lagoon looked choppier than usual today, as did the inlet waters frothing under the high causeway bridge that linked the north and south sides of Comet Cove. So the ocean would be bumpy, too. Were wind and waves a factor in whatever happened to the boat Roz had heard about on the scanner?

Windy or not, it was a beautiful day, cool and sunny, a lot nicer than a late February day in Baltimore would have been. Roz breathed in a lungful of delicious briny air and admired the gleaming yachts and pleasure boats, speedboats and sailboats as she walked toward the pink building that held the office and a shop and snack bar. Just north, looking for a handout, seagulls circled around the tour vessels, the kind that took wannabes out for a day of deep-sea fishing. Farther along were docks for commercial fishing boats. But where were the cops?

Ah, there they were, in the shadow of a cluster of palm trees: two deputies, hands on their duty belts, chattering away on the water side of the marina office.

She plucked her good camera from her bag and got a couple of shots of them talking before they noticed her, then exchanged it for a notebook and approached.

"Duke!" she called out, and the deputy closest to her, with a powerful build and a thick head of golden-brown hair, turned to her and squinted.

"Roz? I heard you were back," he said, his suntanned face breaking into a grin. "Have you been avoiding me?"

"Of course not. It's great to see you, Deputy Dawson," she said, reverting to a more formal address for Duke, one of the guys she used to hang out with at Comet High. "I'm Roz Melander," she added, addressing the other officer, a young female deputy with brown skin and black hair secured in a neat bun. "I'm with the *Courier.*"

"Deputy Byrd," the officer said flatly. Not a fan of the press, Roz presumed.

"So you're here about our explosion?" Duke said as his colleague frowned.

"Is that what it was?" Roz asked. "I heard a noise and then the sirens and something on the scanner, so I thought I'd see what's happening."

"We're still investigating," Deputy Byrd said.

"Of course. I wouldn't publish anything I can't confirm," Roz assured her. "What can you tell me?"

"Nothing official," Deputy Byrd said, eyeing Duke with a "don't you dare" look.

"It's OK, Naya," Duke said to his colleague, shrugging with a smile that would've made Lady Macbeth roll over. He turned to Roz. "Look, if you don't attribute it to one of us, I can tell you a little. We'll get you an official statement later."

"OK. No problem," Roz said. Deputy Byrd sighed.

"The Coast Guard's investigating now," Duke said. "They happened to be in the area and got on site pretty quick. And we've sent our department boat out there, too."

"Out where?" Roz asked.

"In the ocean," he said, "eight miles or so northeast of the inlet. A couple of fishermen called it in after we all heard that bang this morning. Said there was a bunch of smoke, but they didn't want to get too close after they saw all the debris."

"Debris? What kind of debris?" Roz wrote fast, hoping she could decipher her own handwriting later.

"Boat pieces. And I mean *pieces.* So far they haven't found anything bigger than a skateboard. I really doubt there are survivors."

"Any idea who was on board?" Roz had heard the mention of Lunaria Lodge on the radio but wanted to see what Duke said.

"I can't really tell you our theory just yet," he said. "But the Coast Guard was able to find a piece of the hull with a number and part of a name. It looks like the boat was from Consummate Catch."

"That charter fishing tour company that's been marketing itself all over the place?"

To Roz's surprise, Deputy Byrd replied. "That's the one. Based in Bohemia, but they have some boats here. They've been dropping brochures everywhere, including Lunaria Lodge. Apparently rich guys like to fish." Echoing the radio chatter, Naya Byrd's words implied a connection to the resort. Roz considered pressing the deputies to see if they'd admit that Lunaria guests were on board.

But Deputy Byrd's face turned to stone as she looked past Roz.

"Good morning, officers," came a familiar deep voice, and Roz cursed under her breath. She turned to face Alden Knox. "Ms. Melander," he said, nodding at Roz as he stopped beside her.

She said nothing, just tried to ignore the way the morning sun defined the captivating angles of his face. The way her stupid heart gave a little leap. She really had to cut down on the caffeine.

"So I gather there was an exploding boat this morning," Alden said, jumping right in. "Was someone from Lunaria Lodge on board?"

Roz frowned, and Duke suddenly became less talkative. "We won't have that information until the families have been notified. If there are casualties, that is."

"I'm told there were at least two deaths," Alden said.

*Is he bluffing?* It was Roz's turn to scowl. *What's his source?* And then she realized that Duke had said "families." If Alden had concluded what she did from the radio chatter, and if multiple families had to be notified, then at least two people were dead. Astute on Alden's part, she had to admit.

"Like I said, we won't know anything until later this afternoon. The Coast Guard is investigating now," Duke said to Alden. "Who are you with again?"

"My apologies. Alden Knox with *The Beacon.*" He peered at the deputies' name tags. "Nice to meet you, Deputy Dawson, Deputy Byrd. Anything you can tell me? What caused the explosion?"

"You'll find out when we do, I suppose," Duke said, politely obtuse. "I was just telling *Ms. Melander* here that we won't have a statement until later." He grinned at Roz. "Maybe we can get a cone sometime, Roz."

Ah. Duke still remembered her weakness for ice cream, their inevitable dessert during a series of pleasant but platonic high school dates. Out of the corner of her eye, she saw Alden frown at her inside track. She just smiled. The only relationship she wanted with Duke, er, Deputy Dawson, was professional.

"We'll have to talk about that. Great to see you," she told Duke. "And to meet you," Roz said to Deputy Byrd. She nodded at the officers, completely ignored Alden and walked back to her car. She spared one glance over her shoulder to see the deputies retreating to the marina office, abandoning Alden on the docks.

He had balls, walking right into the middle of her interview. And why did he call her Ms. Melander? Of course, Duke had picked it up, teasing her, making her feel about twice her thirty-two years.

Roz shook it off, got in her car and headed back to the office to make a phone call. They'd given her some good color, practically confirmed at least two belateds and dropped the name of the fishing charter. That was a hell of a start.

ALDEN STOOD there for a moment in the swishing shadows of the palm fronds, wondering if he should follow the cops. They'd vanished into the squat pink building.

He thought not. If that hadn't been a dismissal, he didn't know what was. He wasn't ready to irritate them beyond all cooperation. That could come later, when his need was greater. He knew how to pick his battles.

And apparently, he was in a battle with Ms. Melander— Roz, as her chummy deputy had called her. Of course they'd be chummy. She grew up here, his editor had told him, and her family founded the *Courier*.

They still looked pretty chummy, her and the cop. Or did she blow him off there at the end? Deputy Dawson had covertly eyed her, head to toe, as she'd left. Who could blame him, given how those clingy gray trousers and soft coral sweater caressed her curves?

Oh, hell, this was not productive. So the locals wouldn't give him the time of day. Yet he had something to go on. He'd overheard them mention a fishing charter. He hadn't gotten the name. Still, a charter apparently went out with at least one guest from the Lunaria Lodge on board. So there could be two or more victims.

He honestly wasn't thrilled about writing about dead people. Death never made him happy. He genuinely hoped it was no more than two stiffs. For now, he needed to figure out if any of them was Somebody, someone the world would care about. Or click on.

Alden wandered back to the marina lot and walked the rows of cars, packed with mostly upscale vehicles, along with a few beaters that probably belonged to professional fishermen and the like. He looked for anything out of the ordinary. The deceased guest might have gotten a ride. He might be driving a rental. Then again—

*Holy cannoli.*

There wasn't another car like this one in the lot. There might not be another one like it in Florida. It was a convertible, top up, with the slouching, curvy lines of a classic British roadster. Its caramel-brown leather seats and vintage-inspired details contrasted beautifully with its gleaming, deep blue finish. He leaned over the back to look at the winged logo. Morgan. An Aero 8.

It had California plates. Of course, the owner had probably sent it via transport, rather than driving it across the country. Rich people had better things to do than actually drive their insanely posh cars. Alden, on the other hand, would love to drive a car like this across the country. Get away. Find America. Maybe next to a beautiful woman with chestnut hair.

*Think,* Alden told himself. *Who would have a car like this?*

Then it clicked. He'd heard rumors, but it was hard to believe an actor that big would come to this admittedly beautiful backwater, even if it had become a celebrity magnet. Then again, the actor in question—a noted car collector—had endured a highly publicized breakup with his equally famous girlfriend, who now had a girlfriend of her own. If a famous guy wanted to get away from the hype machine, Comet Cove was the place to do it. Especially if he wanted to rest up before filming his next blockbuster espionage thriller.

Still, it was hard to be sure.

He looked at the license plate again.

"Idiot," Alden murmured to himself. Upon first glance, he hadn't even read the vanity moniker there: SPYBOY.

Now he had no doubt. Or, at least, not enough to stop him from posting a speculative scoop. The religion of *The Beacon* was this: It was better to be first than to be right. Still, he leaned over the Aero 8's windshield, found the VIN on the dash and recited the number into his phone's notes so he could look it up later. He snapped a few photos of the car, too.

Alden's spine prickled when he realized just how big the story was going to be, probably bigger than anything he'd ever penned for the *National Eye*.

At least he couldn't ruin the life of his subject this time. The man was already dead.

# chapter
**three**

"HI. This is Roz Melander from the *Comet Cove Courier.* Could I please speak to Mr. Verret?"

Back at her desk, Roz scrolled through Consummate Catch's website while she waited to be connected to the president. His name was online, along with a lot more information. Apparently the company wasn't just into fishing charters. It did commercial fishing, too, priding itself on environmentally friendly methods as it provided some of the area's top restaurants with fresh Atlantic seafood. Her stomach growled. It was just about lunchtime, and she suddenly had a craving for scampi.

She'd already written up a short story but didn't want to post it online until she got a confirmation from the fishing company. And so she waited, taking an unpleasant sip of her mocha, watered down with melted ice after it sat on her desk all morning.

Around her were mostly empty desks. Bruce, the pale, fresh-out-of-college Comet Cove native with electrified short black hair who handled sports, was also on the phone. Janice, who handled community and school news, was out covering a robotics competition at the high school. Roz mostly wrote hard news, but they all penned features and crossed beats as needed.

At the moment, the only other person in their small office was her superhero office manager, Kerry, whose desk was tucked behind a counter at the front door. The small business staff had gone out to lunch to celebrate Trixie getting a new job in Bohemia. Roz knew Trixie wasn't the only one sending out resumes around here, given the state of the *Courier*.

She tried to ignore the hold music—which sounded like a ukulele cover of "Margaritaville"—and tapped idly in her notes file on the laptop. *Alden Knox eaten by shark. Reporter's tragic end in Star Harbor …*

"This is Peter Verret."

Startled after the long hold, Roz almost dropped the phone at the sound of his clipped voice. She tapped the erase key, deleting Alden's demise, as she spoke.

"Mr. Verret, I work for the *Courier* here in Comet Cove. I'm writing a story about a boat explosion that happened offshore this morning. I'm told that one of your boats may be involved, and I wondered if you could confirm that information?"

There was silence for a moment. Roz kept her mouth shut, knowing silence often compelled the other party to speak.

"Yes, sadly, one of our boats was lost this morning," he said.

She tried not to reveal how relieved she was that he answered the question. "How many people were on board?"

"I don't think that's any of your business."

*Ouch.* So that was how this was going to go.

"I'm very sorry for your loss, sir, but we want to be as accurate as possible in the newspaper story. Were there any survivors?"

"Listen," Verret said. "This was a tragic event for our company. We're like a family here. We hope there are survivors. The search isn't over yet. I've deployed two more of my boats to help, but the devastation was terrible. One of our most promising young guides was on board. That's all I'm going to say."

"But you had at least one guest on board—"

*Click.*

"Rude," Roz muttered. She'd just have to polish what she had and get it online.

"Uh, Roz?" It was Bruce, no longer on the phone.

"Yeah?"

"Have you seen the *Beacon* website?"

The look on Bruce's face wasn't encouraging. Oh, no. Not Alden Knox.

"Crap," she muttered, clicking the *Beacon* bookmark in her browser, loading her rival's much more colorful site.

A publicity still from the movie *Spy Match 3* led the page, showing an actor she'd recognize anywhere leaping off a skyscraper as it exploded in a wall of orange flame and smoke. Below it screamed the headline:

### SUPERSTAR BOYD BELLAMY
### POSSIBLE VICTIM IN BOAT EXPLOSION

"Where the heck did he get *that?*" Roz exclaimed.

Bruce cowered. Roz lowered her voice.

"Nothing was said about Hollywood's golden boy being on that boat!" she ranted. "Are they just making stuff up over there?"

"The story doesn't say much else," Bruce pointed out.

"Because he doesn't have anything. He'll get a zillion hits, and then he'll take it all down and write what really happened." But Roz had a sick feeling. She didn't think Alden Knox would publish a headline that inflammatory without some idea that it was true, even if he was Mr. Tabloid. Oh, yeah, she'd googled him. She'd seen his "work" in the *National Eye.*

At least it said "possible victim." Alden didn't know for sure, either.

Roz looked up. Janice, newly arrived, hovered by their cluster of desks, her eyes wide at Roz's outburst.

"Problem?" Janice asked.

"*The Beacon*," Roz grumbled.

Janice smiled and sat, dropping her big bag next to her desk. She wore black pants, a white blouse and a red linen jacket that complemented her light brown skin, accented by a chunky necklace that probably had its origins in her mom's nearby shop, The Bead Blast. Her hair was parted into pretty poufs of black twist-curls, and her brown eyes twinkled in amusement.

"Is it that hottie?" Janice asked.

"Argh," Roz replied.

"So it is him. Alden Knox, right? I got the alert on my phone. Heck of a story."

"Then you know I have a lot of catching up to do," Roz said. "How were the kids' robots?"

"Amazing," Janice said, pulling her laptop and a camera out of her bag. "We're all doomed."

Bruce snorted and went back to his computer as Roz turned back to her desk.

More composed, Roz dialed Consummate Catch again,

waiting even longer this time to be connected with Peter Verret. The music had moved on to steel drums, putting her in mind of a headache-inducing weekend cruise she'd once taken to the Bahamas that had put her off frozen red drinks forever. She was just about to give up hope when he picked up the phone.

"Mr. Verret, Roz Melander. I'm sorry to disturb you again, but I absolutely have to ask you a question to make sure our story is accurate and responsible."

"That seems unlikely," he said, but he didn't hang up.

"There's a report that Boyd Bellamy was on your boat. Can you confirm?"

"This is something you'll have to ask the Coast Guard."

"You know who was on your boat, I presume?" Roz winced at her own tone, but she hated to be stonewalled.

"Yes," he said, more snippy. "But the victims—I mean, families have to be notified. The search is still going on."

"I'm not asking if he was killed, sir. Just if he was on board. Can you confirm?"

"No."

"Can you deny it?"

Another pause. "No."

"If I publish a story that said he was on board your boat, would I be wrong?"

Roz heard a mumble, as if he'd covered up the receiver on the other end and was talking to someone else.

After a moment, Verret came back on. "Mr. Bellamy was scheduled to be on our boat out of Star Harbor this morning. That's all I can confirm at this time."

"Thank you!" Roz said, wincing at her own enthusiasm. "Why do you think your boat exploded?"

*Click.*

"Rats." It didn't matter. Not yet. At least she had some kind of confirmation. She'd get it online in two minutes, with better information and better sourcing than *The Beacon.*

Even if *he* had beaten her to the story.

ALDEN HAD to hand it to Roz (demoted from Ms. Melander now that he knew her nickname). He'd beaten her to the biggest scoop, but she'd been hot on his tail with a confirmation and multiple sources. Now he needed something to push the story forward.

This afternoon's police statement hadn't added much to what he'd already learned, except that it confirmed only two people were on board the obliterated boat: the fishing guide and Boyd Bellamy. The Coast Guard was investigating the accident—that's what they were calling it—but no one had suggested what caused it.

Alden's cynical journalistic mind suspected that more was going on, or maybe he just hoped it was. A boring fishing trip and, say, a cantankerous engine didn't sound like much of a story. He wanted to recreate the star's last day or so on Earth, and if there was something dark and dangerous about his little fishing expedition, he wanted to know that, too.

The place to start was Bellamy's last known hideaway, Lunaria Lodge.

Alden navigated from his office through downtown to A1A,

then turned south, enjoying the drive. Comet Cove had a charm that blended seaside kitsch and art and now a whiff of glamour as it became an escape for the famous who were stressed out by LA pressure, traffic and snap-happy stalkers.

He privately worried that the charm that attracted him and now the stars might turn this place into an Aspen or a Miami Beach, a super-rich enclave that was no more than a mini Hollywood. Only with hurricanes instead of earthquakes. It remained to be seen.

He'd even heard rumors of someone building a small movie studio at the far south end of Comet Cove, somewhere near the airfield, but he still didn't have enough facts to publish a story. And his standards for publishing were low, he had to admit. He'd track that down when he put this boat story to bed.

In a few minutes, he reached the bridge and soared over Star Inlet to the south side of town. Even his cynical heart couldn't help a leap at the gorgeous view, the sparkling water beneath him and half of Comet Cove laid out beyond. It felt like flying as he sped across the causeway. And then he was back among the beachy retail along the highway before he took the left at the light onto Lighthouse Road.

He slowed down for the curvy, palm-lined lane along the waterway that led to Stargazer Point. Large houses to his right nestled among tropical foliage, oaks and palms. To his left, those properties' palatial docks sported impressive boats that seemed to exist more as a billboard for the wealth of their owners than for actual recreation and transportation.

In less than a mile, a tasteful wooden sign on the right indicated the entrance to Lunaria Lodge. As he made the turn, he glimpsed the lighthouse off to his left, on the very eastern end of the point.

Driving among the trees of the resort, he immediately felt sheltered from the world, in touch with nature, and safely in the hands of professionals who knew how to cosset their well-heeled guests. Once a guest got out into the cruel world—well, there was no telling what would happen. And it seemed that poor Boyd Bellamy's fishing line had run out.

Amid the stunning landscaping, Lunaria's guest cottages mingled with amenities—a tennis court, a swimming pool, a spa—until he arrived at a parking lot of paver stones behind the three-story main building. He could've gone valet, but he preferred to have keys in hand, just in case he needed to leave in a hurry.

The lodge mimicked an overgrown cabin of logs interspersed with stucco, with grand windows taking advantage of the spectacular view of the sea. But in the way of Florida's theme parks, the "wood trim" seemed to be mostly made of cleverly sculpted concrete. The faux cabin's walls of russet and cream gleamed in the mellow light of late afternoon.

Besides guest rooms, the main building held a restaurant and bar. The bar patio, left of the main entrance, overlooked the beach. Dotted with umbrella tables, it was already busy with happy guests. The restaurant featured a second-floor deck as well.

Alden preferred the dark, cool inside bar to the party patio, but he resisted the temptation. He wasn't ready to go in and seek an official interview. Not yet. He wanted to explore behind the scenes.

He walked deeper into the resort, on a secluded stone path surrounded by palm trees, hibiscus, sea grapes and flowering bushes. He saw little activity between the stucco guest cottages, only a cluster of laughing young women. Where were they going? The beach? No. Maybe the spa. They had that bridesmaid aura about them, fresh and young and unspoiled by life. He almost remembered what that was like. He nodded at them appreciatively, and they smiled back at him. Women usually did.

He caught a maid coming out of one of the cottages, pushing a cart laden with towels and potions, and asked her which way the restaurant was. He already knew, but it was an easy question for her to answer. And then he asked her where Boyd Bellamy was staying.

"I can't talk about any of our guests," the young redhead said, caution creeping into her voice.

"It's a shame what happened to him. I thought I might leave some flowers," Alden said.

"You don't have any flowers."

"I thought I'd pick a few hibiscus, something in the spirit of the place."

She shook her head, looking around nervously. "The landscapers aren't going to like it if you start snipping the plants, sir."

"How long had Mr. Bellamy been staying at the resort?" Alden turned his most bewitching smile on the young woman. "He's gone now. You telling me can't possibly harm him."

"He got here Sunday," she murmured after another pause. "I wasn't in charge of cleaning his cottage, though. I don't know anything else."

Sunday. It was Wednesday. So the actor had only been here a few days. "What did he like to do?"

"Well, the other girls said he liked to fish on the beach. He would go for a run in the morning. Some of us would watch for him—oh, this is so embarrassing. Why do you want to know?"

"I—"

"Erin!" came a piercing male voice from behind him, interrupting his explanation. Which he hadn't invented quite yet. "Jupiter Cottage needs a fresh set of towels. See to it, won't you?"

Alden turned to see a narrow-nosed pale man with thinning light brown hair and a tiny mustache walking toward them, wearing a cream linen suit and pink tie. He waved a tablet computer at the hapless maid. Alden had a feeling Jupiter Cottage's towels weren't the issue. He was.

"Yes, of course, Mr. Frankel," Erin said. "Just telling this gentleman where the restaurant was." She snuck a brief smile at Alden before heading off with her cart.

"I see," Mr. Frankel said. "May I help you, sir?"

Alden perceived that this tablet-brandishing rule-enforcer must be some kind of manager. He doubted he'd get much out of him, but it was worth a try.

"I'm Alden Knox from *The Beacon,*" he said, approaching Frankel, looking for the right words to keep Erin the maid out of trouble. "Miss Erin was just giving me directions, but perhaps you might be able to answer a few questions?"

Frankel registered that Alden was press, and his whole demeanor changed from stiff martinet to a kind of cautious politeness. "Good afternoon, sir. Do you need more guidance on where the restaurant is?"

"I think I've figured it out," Alden said with an arch smile. "I wanted to know a little more about Boyd Bellamy. Did he have any guests here at Lunaria Lodge? How did he spend his days?"

Frankel's posture turned rigid again. "We do not discuss our guests, especially with the press. If you have any questions, you may direct them to the police or Mr. and Mrs. Reyes. Inquire at the lodge. The main building."

"But I just—"

"The restaurant, should you still require it, is inside the lodge, and it's excellent." Frankel approximated a smile and pointed over Alden's shoulder.

"Thank you," Alden said with a polite nod before turning on his heel and heading back toward the lodge. He gritted his teeth. The staff might be a little too good here.

Mr. and Mrs. Reyes—that would be Diego and Liani, the owners of the place. He'd met them at a charity luncheon he'd covered here. Maybe he could get them to answer a few questions.

The big lobby soared under a high atrium that let in natural light, with overlooks on the second and third floors where a few guests perched at railings and watched people come and go. Along one wall, a huge stone fireplace looked like something out of a western ski lodge, not the Florida tropics, but somehow it worked with the wood-look tile floor and tropical plants. Gas flames flickered around ceramic logs on the hearth, and all the comfy chairs around it were occupied. Signs pointed to the bar and restaurant—he could hear its chatter from here—along with a ballroom, a game room and elevators.

He walked straight to the reception desk, where he saw just the woman he wanted to talk to: Liani Reyes, her dark hair pinned up, her brown eyes shining. Pretty woman. And so was the guest she spoke to.

*Oh, crap.*

The "guest" was Roz Melander.

To his gratification, Liani shook her head, her smile fading to a frown, as she spoke to Roz. "I'm afraid that's all we can say. It's a tragic thing," Alden heard as he approached the counter. "I will tell you that I've pulled all the brochures for

Consummate Catch until we find out just what caused the accident."

"Wise move," Roz said, and then she froze, her graceful shoulders arrested in a straight line. She turned slowly.

"Ms. Melander," Alden said with almost abject civility and a slight bow.

"Would you stop calling me that, Mr. Knox?"

"It's your name, isn't it?"

"Well, I'll just let you two talk," Liani said, a smile quirking at the corner of her mouth. She turned and disappeared through a door behind the counter, letting another clerk check in arriving guests.

"I wanted to talk to her," Alden told Roz, this time letting his annoyance shine through.

"As if she would tell you more than she told me."

"Women often do."

"Cad," Roz said, stuffing her notebook into her purse. Something was written on it. He was dying to know what.

"You don't know enough about me to call me a cad."

"Oh, I'm sure knowing more would only underscore the point."

"Undeniably," Alden said, flashing briefly on the gut-wrenching events that had pushed him to give up the kind of Girl Scout journalism she seemed to espouse.

Roz paused and cocked her head, considering him.

Alden tried not to squirm under her scrutiny; instead he let himself be distracted by her shifting chestnut hair. Red highlights in the long strands caught the indirect soft glow from the sunlit ocean, a gilded beachscape he could see through the lobby windows.

"Looks like a beautiful sunset. Why don't you join me for

dinner?" The words came out of his mouth before he could stop them. What the hell was he doing?

She harrumphed. "I've been craving Chef Sofia's scampi all day, but it won't taste as good if I'm having dinner with you."

"Now, be fair," Alden said. "You don't even know me. And if you're trying to pump the wait staff for information, it will look a lot less suspicious if you have a date. You know, if you appear to be a regular curious person and not a terrifying journalist."

"I am not terrifying." Roz straightened, throwing her shoulders back, which had the glorious effect of pushing her perfect breasts out. As he took a heartbeat to appreciate her figure, a light flashed in her amber, green-flecked eyes. Could that spark be—interest?

No. Couldn't be. But he felt a flush of heat just the same, and not just because he hadn't dated in weeks. What part of him thought asking this impossible woman to dinner was a good idea? Certainly not a part with a brain.

There was just something about her. She wasn't a conventional beauty, exactly, but she had a kind of girl-next-door glamour that made him want to be her neighbor.

"What do you say?" Alden prodded, unable to help himself. "I was going to eat here, too. Let's be friends."

"Fat chance," Roz said. "But you do make sense. I mean, about looking suspicious. People will say anything to you if they think you're *not* a journalist. Not that I would ever go into an interview without identifying myself, but dinner ..."

"Relax. This isn't an ethics investigation. If it were, you'd pass with flying colors, I'm sure."

"And you?" she asked.

"You'd be horrified," Alden said. "Shall we?"

## chapter
# five

ROZ EYED ALDEN with suspicion and not a little lust as he talked the hostess into seating them at a primo table on the second level, up the curvy open staircase and by large windows overlooking the Atlantic Ocean. The man was a charmer, despite his protestations of ill repute.

The place was surprisingly busy for a Wednesday night, both inside and outside on the second-floor deck. Sirenia's fine food and ambience had attracted the attention of diners not just on Comet Cove, but from towns up and down the coast. Roz had been to Sirenia only a few times—Taco Titan was more in her budget—but every meal she'd had here had been delightful.

So was the scenery. Feathery clouds lit up orange as the sky deepened into purple over the shimmering sea, framed by clusters of palm trees.

She and Alden perused their menus, pretending to ignore each other. They both looked up as their server arrived at the table.

"Lily?" Roz asked, surprised to see her morning barista wearing black and looking official. "You work here, too?"

"Oh, hi, Roz. Yeah, it helps to have two jobs when you're saving for nursing school. And"—the blonde smiled nervously as she turned to Alden—"I've never actually learned your name, sir."

"Alden Knox from *The Beacon*. My fault for not introducing myself before now. I get nervous in the presence of beautiful women."

Roz rolled her eyes as Lily lit up at Alden's flirting.

"*The Beacon?*" Lily shot Roz, aka the *Courier*, a puzzled look, then turned back to Alden with a besotted grin. "Nice to meet you. I mean, see you. Now let me tell you about our specials. We have a wonderful tomino e prosciutto di parma, which is an Italian cheese wrapped in imported ham and grilled, with pecans and a sweet fig reduction. If you like cheese, we have a very nice Italian cheese board to start; the Pecorino di Pienza is my favorite. And our fish of the day is cobia. Do you have any questions about the menu?"

"Actually, I have a question about the wine list," Alden said. "I'm a fan of the nerellos, but I don't see any on the list—do you happen to have one in your cellar?"

"I'll check," Lily said. "We have quite a few wines that aren't on the list, in case Chef Sofia gets a whim. I'll be right back."

Lily left while Roz's finger was still in midair, in the "hail waitress" pose. So much for a quick dinner and an early night before her secret expedition in the morning.

"Are you a wine snob?" she asked Alden. "And what's a nerello?"

"A type of grape," he said. "I discovered them in Sicily a few years ago when I tacked on a vacation after stalking a certain megastar for a week up at Lake Como."

"Lake Como?" Roz figured she knew which star, then. A

very hot one. Even hotter than Alden. *Stop it,* she told herself before adding, "Nothing like roughing it."

"Turns out, back before his marriage, this star didn't mind letting you think you'd squeezed him for gossip if he drank with you for a couple of hours and got to prank you afterward. After I thought I got my scoop from him and his buddies, I left the Grand Hotel Tremezzo to find my rented Smart car wedged sideways between two tour buses in the lakefront parking lot."

Roz laughed in spite of herself. "Serves you right."

"It was still a story, even if he had one over on me," Alden said with a shrug. "And in Italy, it's hard to mind. *La dolce vita* and all that."

Lily returned to the table, accompanied by a petite woman Roz recognized: Chef Sofia, in a short-sleeved black chef jacket. Her short black hair held a streak of pink, and her arms danced with colorful tattoos, including intertwined art of spaghetti, basil and tomatoes.

Chef Sofia offered up a bottle of wine and spoke with a delightful Italian accent. "I heard the local press were dining with us, and I wanted to say ciao. Nice to see you, Roz."

*So much for going incognito.* "It's great to see you, too," she told the chef. "Alden Knox, this is Chef Sofia Costa."

"Very pleased to meet you," Alden said in silken tones, standing to shake the chef's hand.

"Grazie," Sofia said, motioning him back into his chair. "I admit, I was curious to see who was interested in a nerello. I think you'll like this. On the house." She handed the bottle to Lily, and she proceeded to open it.

"You don't have to do that!" Roz mentally calculated the symbolic debt she'd owe Sofia for the wine.

"Very kind of you," Alden told the chef, ignoring Roz's protest. "What can you tell us about it?"

"It's a nerello mascalese. Something about the volcanic soil gives it a beautiful bite." Sofia shot an impish look at Alden as Lily poured a small sip of the Tasca d'Almerita vintage for him to try.

Roz sat back, crossed her arms and watched, annoyed at Alden's presumption in accepting the wine but fascinated at the way he breathed deeply from the glass, swirled the light red liquid, closed his eyes, sipped and savored. It was as if he were slipping into a dream. She bit off a sigh as she watched him.

"Excellent," Alden said, opening those clear gray eyes.

"I couldn't agree more," Sofia said. "I'd better go back to the kitchen. By the way, I recommend the cobia. It's hard to get this time of year, but we have a lovely batch."

The chef waved and headed back to the kitchen as Lily filled their wineglasses. Alden ordered the cobia, and Roz ordered the scampi she'd been craving all day. When Lily left, Roz frowned at her dinner mate.

"Way to blow our cover," she said.

"Our server knew who we were."

"She knew who *I* was, but she didn't know you were press, too, until you made a point of it, and now the chef has probably told everyone in the kitchen."

"That doesn't mean everyone here knows who we are. Maybe we'll find someone else to babble about Bellamy. Try the wine. It's divine." Alden took a long sip and smiled.

"You're incorrigible," Roz said, just as Lily dropped off a cheese board they hadn't ordered and skittered off again. "What the——?"

"It's a perk. Let it go," Alden said.

"Not for me. I don't take freebies. I don't want it to look like I'm giving somebody good coverage just because they're feeding me."

"Don't worry. By the time you're done with the story about the exploding movie star, no one will think you're taking it easy on this place."

Roz shook her head. "The lodge isn't involved."

"You're so sure?"

"It was an accident. Probably lousy safety standards on the part of Consummate Catch." She watched hungrily as Alden popped a piece of the cheese and a thin slice of prosciutto between his delectable lips, making an "Mmmm" sound that notched up her body heat five degrees.

"We'll see where it leads us," he said. "Have some cheese."

"There is no 'us' when it comes to this story." Roz eyed the cheese, sighed and took a piece. "I guess I'll just leave an enormous tip."

Alden chuckled. "That's the spirit."

She sipped the wine. "Oh, my. That's good, too."

"Told you."

"Hope it doesn't cost too much."

"Retails for forty dollars, give or take. They probably charge a hundred twenty or so for it here."

Roz almost choked on the olive she'd popped into her mouth. *"What?"*

"Enjoy it. If you're that worried about it, I'll insist on paying for the wine."

"Salaries must be a lot higher at *The Beacon* than they are at the *Courier*."

"I'm fairly certain they are." She wanted to slap Alden's look of amusement off his face, except that it was so—delicious. Almost as delicious as the wine and cheese.

"So what's your angle?" Alden asked.

"I'll know when I figure it out," Roz said, then bit her lip for giving away that much.

Was it her imagination, or did his gaze linger on her lips when she did that?

The wine must be going to her head. She kind of liked it. She poured herself some more.

"I'm not trying to poach your story," he said. "You can write the hard-hitting tirade about the shoddy boats and the threat to tourism, and I'll write about Bellamy's agonizing last minutes and the brokenhearted starlets he leaves behind."

"That's pretty harsh." Roz looked out the windows, where the purple twilight was fading into night. Where the water held so many secrets. "From what I've heard, the guy was pretty brokenhearted himself."

"So you do read celebrity gossip." A mischievous smile played about his mouth.

"I live in America. I pretty much get celebrity gossip via osmosis." Plus she'd spent half the afternoon researching Boyd Bellamy and his ugly breakup.

"I have friends in lawyers' offices in L.A."

"So?" Roz tried not to sound too curious but leaned forward involuntarily.

"So I know something you don't."

"How can you be sure?"

"I'm sure," Alden said, refilling his own wineglass and chasing a chunk of cheese with a fresh sip. She watched him, refusing to bite, waiting for him to fill the silence. He raised an elegant eyebrow. She waited some more. He smiled. "So I'll tell you what I know if you tell me what Mrs. Reyes told you."

"Ah," Roz said, leaning back, smiling in turn, playing poker. Her hand was pretty lame, but he didn't need to know that.

"You won't tell me?"

"How can I be sure what I know is worth what you know?"

He leaned forward, his elbows on the table, and spoke softly. "Because what I know could make this a murder mystery."

"Get *out*," she said, unable to hide her excitement. She mentally kicked herself and tried to sound calm again. "I don't know if I believe you. How about you go first."

Alden leaned into her space for another minute, his eyes glinting, then sat back and took another sip of wine. "Boyd Bellamy never changed his will after he and Mysty Wellington broke up."

"The supermodel? So?"

"So he left a scandalously huge estate to her, even when it appears they hated each other."

"Really." Roz considered the information as Lily delivered their food and left. She took a bite of the buttery, garlicky shrimp and couldn't suppress a small sound of satisfaction. She caught Alden watching her with a hint of something that looked like hunger. "It could be coincidence. They haven't been apart that long. Maybe he just hadn't gotten around to changing the will."

"Exactly," Alden said. "Maybe she had to act before he had a *chance* to change it."

"So she arranges an explosion in the middle of the ocean that also kills a fishing guide? I don't buy it. I don't know a lot of famous people, but she doesn't strike me as the type."

"God, this fish is good," Alden said, chasing a mouthful with wine. "And I do know a lot of famous people, and let me assure you, what you see is most definitely not what you get. Virtually all of them wear a mask at all times."

"Because of 'journalists' like you," Roz said with a smirk.

"I heard those quotation marks, and I'm not offended," he said, though he sounded as if he was. "Did you know TMZ has three reporters stationed at the L.A. courthouse, while the *Los Angeles Times* has just one? As a reporter and editor for the *Eye,* I had sources everywhere. I had a team that could tear apart legal documents for the most astounding facts. It was journalism, my dear, even if it wasn't your type of journalism. Speaking of which, just what did you learn from Liani Reyes?"

Roz shifted in her chair, uncomfortable after Alden's dressing-down and, in spite of herself, a little sorry that she'd insulted him. Maybe he had a point, even if their styles were about as different as wrestlers in high school and wrestlers sparkling in sequins as they pounded mats on TV.

Now she leaned forward, and Alden did, too, forcing her eyes to meet his crystal gaze. As a bonus, she got a whiff of his pleasant scent.

*Focus, Roz, focus.*

She kept her voice low. "Liani let it drop that they had to cancel a special-order carriage ride Bellamy had scheduled for tomorrow."

Alden sat up with a loud laugh that made her want to laugh, too, even if it was at her expense. "A carriage ride?"

"Shhh," Roz said, looking around. They hadn't drawn much attention, as far as she could see. She looked back at Alden as he took another big bite of his fish. "Don't you get it? A man doesn't go for a carriage ride by himself. He takes a woman with him—or, you know, whatever he's into. He had a date."

Alden chewed and swallowed, drank more wine and contemplated her. Roz drank more, too, waiting for him to respond, feeling the first hint of a buzz, wondering why she was sharing information with this wickedly handsome man. Or simply *wicked* man.

"I grant you the point," he finally said. "It could be worth a follow-up, if only to write about the tragedy of having to cancel his momentous date."

"We should talk to the director of the carriage company. I got the name."

"I thought 'we' were not pursuing this story together?"

"We're not," Roz said. "But I know you're going to find them anyway, so we might as well bother them at the same time. And I don't feel like racing you there first thing in the morning." *Because I have something else to do,* she thought.

"That sounds reasonable. Our audiences are different, anyway. Mine is more national. You should see our web traffic."

"You don't have to sound so smug about it," she said, and Alden chuckled. There she was, on the defensive again. She had to get out of here.

Lily returned to the table as they finished their entrees. "Any room for dessert?"

"Not for me," Roz said. "Can you split the check?"

"One check," Alden said with authority. "I'll take it. And Lily, please make sure you put the wine on there. My ethics prevent me from accepting it as a gift." He turned toward Roz with a serious look and a mocking raised eyebrow.

*Argh!* "But I shouldn't let you pay—"

"Our coffers are deep, Ms. Melander." Alden dribbled the last of the wine into his glass and knocked it back as Lily left the folder on the table. Roz caught a glimpse of the bill and gulped as he inserted a credit card into the folder and snapped it shut. He sat back, watching Roz.

She crossed her arms. "You're a piece of work."

"And an excellent piece of ... work, I'm told."

She huffed. "I would've split the wine with you."

"We did split the wine," he said.

"I mean the cost! What about the cheese?"

"You said you'd leave a big tip," he said. "I'll allow that."

Roz shook her head, pulled out her wallet and shoved some cash onto the table. *Ouch.* Even that was going to cut into her food budget.

Alden spoke after Lily picked up the folder and left again. "Shall we go ask people what they know about Boyd Bellamy? Maybe try the bar patio?"

"Honestly? I've had enough of Boyd Bellamy for one day," Roz said. "But I want to take a walk and get some air before I drive home. We can talk tomorrow about the carriage."

"I have nowhere to be," Alden said. "I'll walk with you."

Roz glowered at him. "You don't have to spy on me, Mr. Knox. I'm not going to get any precious scoops walking on the beach in the dark."

"You know, I like it when you call me Mr. Knox." His eyes, his tone were full of mischief, and Roz's face got hot. Lily returned with the check, and he signed and got up. "Shall we?"

Roz wasn't used to being this muddled. A moment ago, she hated this man. But now part of her was all too ready to join him.

"All right." She felt OK, but a walk on the beach would freshen her up and help her digest this decadent meal. "Let me put my purse in the car."

A few minutes later, with her keys in her pocket and her shoes left next to Alden's by the walkway, she reluctantly joined him in a stroll to the water's edge.

# chapter
## six

ALDEN, fueled by a good wine, a good meal and the most entertaining conversation he'd had in months, nonetheless found himself low on words as he escorted Roz to the quiet beach of Lunaria Lodge. A gibbous moon rode high in the sky, touching the waves with silver. Off to the northeast, at the end of Stargazer Point, the lighthouse winked.

A fresh, almost chilly breeze whipped through his hair, and Roz crossed and rubbed her arms.

"Are you cold?" he asked. "I don't have a jacket, but I could give you my shirt."

She looked at him as if he was crazy. "And you would have no shirt."

"I'm hot enough to survive in an undershirt. Would you mind?" He grinned. He couldn't help flirting with her. It seemed to make her so discombobulated.

"I'm fine," she said, shaking out her arms and throwing back her shoulders.

Alden blinked at the sight of her profile in the moonlight and had to think of exploding fishermen to get his thoughts under control.

He turned to her again as they walked, enveloped by the rushing sounds of the water and the night. "Are you drunk?"

"No," Roz said. "I had a bit of a buzz a while ago, but the meal and time took care of that. You'll know it when I'm really drunk."

"Really? I can't wait."

She shot him another look. "Not that you'll get the chance."

"Oh, come on. What are you like when you're drunk?"

"Loquacious. Full of ten-dollar words. I'm like a walking game of Scrabble, with an opinion about everything. Incredibly annoying."

"Sounds delightful. When I'm drunk, I want to be around beautiful women." Alden caught her gaze and imagined starlight in those hazel eyes for a fleeting moment. Maybe he was the one who was drunk.

"I don't get drunk often. It has to be a special occasion. My dad enjoyed his alcohol a little too much when he got going, and sometimes it got him into trouble. I'd rather not be a good-time girl, though I enjoy wine."

"I think you're a good time sober, too," Alden teased, trying and failing to provoke a smile. "I understand your parents founded the *Courier?*"

"Actually, the previous generation did, but my parents served as publisher and editor for years. I grew up in newspapers and never left them, more fool me, so it made sense for me to come back here and help. My dad died over a year ago of a heart attack, and my mom isn't well."

"I'm sorry to hear that. She——?" Alden let his unsaid question hang.

"She has advanced multiple sclerosis. She's not getting better."

"Oh, no."

Roz nodded. "Working at the paper got to be too much for her. She'd like to sell it, but—"

"It's in trouble, isn't it?"

Roz looked up at him, her face cloudy, half-shielded by her windblown hair. "Yes," she admitted.

"No brothers or sisters to help?"

"No one."

"If anyone can save it, you can."

"Ha," she scoffed. "You barely know me."

"I can just tell," Alden said. "But why sell it? Why not just run it?"

"The writing is on the wall," Roz said. "I'd like to sell it while it's still worth something, before newspapers go away, before it's all *Beacon* and gossip." He raised an eyebrow as she continued. "Hopefully someone will buy it and infuse it with new resources. I worry about my staff—my friends. But I'd like a chance to get my job back in Baltimore."

"You were at that scrappy new paper, right?" He'd looked her up, of course. "What did you do there?"

"I'd just made it onto the investigative team when Mom took a turn for the worse. Before that, I covered city government."

"Sounds familiar," Alden murmured.

"What was that?"

"Oh, I once covered city government. Couldn't get out of there fast enough."

"Where?"

"A small town in upstate New York. No place you've ever heard of." Alden didn't want to talk about it, but somehow, he didn't mind her asking.

"Why didn't you like it?"

"Because I screwed it up." Alden stopped. They'd walked so far, the main building was out of sight. A few lights winked from the windows of the resort's premium beachside cottages, half concealed by the tropical foliage. He suddenly wanted to crawl into a hammock under the moon and sleep forever, oblivious to the past.

"What do you mean?" Roz advanced a few steps before realizing he'd stopped, then turned and walked back to face him. Moonlight cast shadows across her features. "What happened?"

"I fulfilled my destiny and became a first-rate tabloid reporter, and I came here, to *The Beacon,* the pinnacle of my journalism career," he said, hearing the acid in his tone. He reeled it back in with a long breath.

"There's a story there."

"Everything's a story," he said.

"And I'm a good reporter."

"I know you are. And I'm *bad*." He tried to sound flirtatious, but her skeptical look stopped him. He tried a half smile instead. "Ready to go back?"

Roz looked him in the eye. "OK," she said softly, and in those two syllables, he heard a sympathy that threatened to cut him wide open. He mentally rebuffed the comfort he might find there.

But as they walked back, Alden considered other forms of comfort. He slipped an arm around her shoulders.

Roz stiffened for a moment, and then she relaxed under his light touch. Her arms were crossed again. She was certainly cold. He pulled her ever so slightly closer. A slow burn ignited in his body at her floral scent—jasmine, he thought—and her proximity. There was something about her that plugged him in, electrified him. He didn't understand it, but he wanted her.

No matter how stupid an idea that might be.

They found their shoes and put them back on, then walked to the parking lot. Alden escorted Roz to her car and watched her unlock and open the door. He held it open, waiting for her to get in. But she didn't. She turned to him.

"We can set up the carriage interview tomorrow," she said. "How about I call? I've met the stable manager before."

"I'm at your disposal."

"Huh," she said, sounding skeptical.

Tomorrow, they'd chase their separate leads again, back to competing. But that was tomorrow. Alden leaned closer, close enough to feel her breath on his face as she looked into his eyes. For a half second, in Roz's canny gaze, anxiety and fatigue warred with something else, something warmer, more subversive.

Alden leaned closer—then sucked in a breath in surprise as Roz ducked into her car.

"Thanks for dinner," she said before she slammed the door. But despite the dismissal, he knew what he'd seen in her eyes. When she stole a glance at him as the car backed out, he saw it again.

Wildfire.

*Holy cannoli.* Roz zoomed off in her little hatchback, and Alden wondered if he'd imagined the whole thing.

He strolled back to his old Miata, his heart and mind racing, wondering what tomorrow would bring.

# chapter
## seven

ROZ WOKE UP GRUMPY, but then, that wasn't unusual these days. There were a lot of reasons: the newspaper's struggles. Her mother's declining health. Obnoxious male journalists who got under her skin.

She cranked up the four-cup coffeemaker in the quaint 1950s kitchen of the bungalow she'd rented. It was down the block from her mother's house in southwest Comet Cove, the house she grew up in.

Her mother had insisted on her getting her own place. "I can't have you always underfoot, watching me all the time, waiting for me to fall over and worrying your face off," she'd said.

So now Roz worried her face off down the block, though she visited her mom often. On the good days, they went out for lunch. On the bad days, her mother curled up in bed and let a part-time home-care aide clean and cook and help her move around the house. Her mother said she hated to have her daughter in the house on those days, but Roz came anyway.

Roz was glad she lived alone on days like today, when she was up at—God, was it really 4:45 a.m.? And after that tête-àtête with her rival last night, the little sleep she did have had been rumpled by dreams she was embarrassed to remember today. Though she couldn't help returning to them again and again: dreams of Alden taking his shirt off on the beach despite her protests, of Alden's eyes flashing in the moonlight, of Alden sweeping her off her feet and—

She shook her head, poured coffee into her go-mug and sweetened it with a couple of teaspoons of sugar. It had been *way* too long. In Baltimore, she dated a nice high school English teacher she'd met when she spoke in his class. Their tepid relationship had made it all too easy to break up when she left six months ago. But he was a good man, and that was the kind of guy she needed to be with. Wasn't it?

Certainly she didn't want an arrogant paparazzo with zero ethics.

But she'd promised Alden that she'd set up an interview with the carriage stable, despite her low hopes for good information.

That would come later. This morning, she wanted to check out the explosion site while it was still fresh, get some color and detail about just what was out there. And maybe clues to why it happened, something the police hadn't told her.

At least she'd gotten the GPS coordinates out of Duke. The probably hopeless search for survivors was supposed to resume once it got light; she wanted to sneak into the area before they got started and have a look around.

She'd donned denim shorts and a sweater over a tank top, hoping she'd look like any other casual boater. Her only concern was the boat.

Roz's family had a twenty-three-footer, but it hadn't been run in months. The boat was twenty-five years old, though her father had replaced the engine and updated the GPS about ten years ago. Her mother hadn't wanted to deal with selling it, but she might have to soon, Roz thought grimly.

Roz wasn't all that handy with boats; her dad was the one who was crazy about fishing. She used to ride with him as a kid but got tired of it later, got interested in other things. So she had almost no knowledge of how the thing worked. But it couldn't be that different from a car, right? She had a key. And she knew the vessel ran. She had a cousin—the son of her dad's brother—who tinkered with it and used it whenever he visited from up north, about twice a year, and he left it fueled every time.

She only had to get eight miles offshore and back. There was no crime scene tape on the ocean. Piece of cake.

Roz told herself all these things, incidentally craving cake, as she made the short drive to Southside Wharf and parked in the predawn darkness. There was no reason she couldn't do this, and it looked as if it was going to be a pretty nice day to be out on the water, less choppy than the day before.

Southside Wharf was the smaller marina in Comet Cove, nestled on the lagoon a few miles south of the inlet, less used and more private than Star Harbor. It lay across the street from a small, woodsy park that was surrounded by neighborhoods. Mostly smaller pleasure and fishing boats docked at Southside, but at the north end, there were larger slips with a few showy vessels and a bigger dock that larger boats sometimes used.

She saw a couple of anglers taking out their boat, smaller than hers. Otherwise it was eerily quiet and chilly as she got out of her car. She grabbed a bag that held her camera and a couple of bottles of water, along with a granola bar, just in case. Then she locked her purse and phone in the trunk, stuffed her keys into a pocket and headed out onto the docks.

The Grady-White, which her dad had dubbed the *Nellie Bly,* looked fine in the minimal harbor lights. Its bimini could use a good cleaning, but it would be enough to keep Roz in the shade when the sun came up for her short trip back home. She tossed her bag on board and climbed in after it, getting oriented. She really hadn't been on this boat since—good lord, had it been a decade?

She found the life preservers and confirmed the radio worked. Her cousin had kept the boat pretty neat. The tiny cabin below and the head were clean, not that she'd be gone long enough to need the toilet, but it paid to be prepared.

Up top, she looked around again and pulled the boat key out of her bag, then secured the bag in a closed compartment. She unhitched the bow line but left the one in back tied to the dock so the boat wouldn't drift while she got it started. Then she stood at the console, put the key in the ignition and turned it.

*Click click click zzzzz*. Nothing happened.

She tried again. Same thing.

Crap. She didn't want to be the dopey girl who couldn't start her boat. Ask her to do any number of other things, and she'd prove she was equal to the task. Dissect a stack of government documents for data? Easy. Assemble IKEA furniture? No problem. But this?

Maybe it was broken.

The last thing she wanted to do was ask for help. She could call her cousin in Cincinnati. It was early, but he might be up at 5:30 a.m. Some people were, right?

"May I be of assistance?"

She whirled, peered into the dim light and found herself staring at the amused face of Alden Knox.

chapter<br>**eight**

"WHAT ARE YOU DOING HERE?" Roz demanded.

Alden held his hands out wide, palms up, wondering if finding her here was lucky or disastrous. "I swear, I didn't know you'd be here."

"Then why are you here?"

"Why are you here? Fishing?" he asked, though it was obvious she wasn't. No gear. No enthusiasm.

She crossed her arms and didn't say anything. In the yellow of the scant wharf lights, she looked ticked off. Par for the course.

And pretty hot, in denim shorts and a dark sweater.

"Aren't you cold?" he asked.

"Stop worrying about my temperature. Why are you here?"

Alden sighed. "I'm meeting a fisherman here. Or I was. He just texted me. He's too hung over to take me out."

"You're going *fishing*," she said in disbelief.

"Apparently not." He was certain they each knew why the other was here. "Can I help you start the boat?"

"Why would you want to do that?"

"Because then you can take me out to the debris field and we can see the accident scene ourselves."

Roz huffed, the sound of frustration and, he hoped, capitulation. She uncrossed her arms. "I don't think this is a good idea."

"We've established we want different things out of the story," Alden said, hopping aboard the boat. He'd worn jeans and a flannel shirt, more fitting to the cool February morning, but he didn't mind looking at Roz's shapely legs. "It won't do any harm. It might even be helpful to have me along."

"I don't see how," Roz said. "Besides, you might ruffle that hundred-dollar haircut."

"I own a convertible. I live to ruffle my haircut. Or have someone ruffle it for me." He shot her a warm look, then scanned the console. "Is this your boat?"

"It used to be my dad's."

"Did you prime the fuel?"

"What?"

Alden grinned and went to the back of the boat. "See this? There's a tube that runs from the gas tank to the engine. You have to squeeze the primer bulb so it gets the fuel moving. You squeeze it until it gets hard."

*"Really."*

He laughed. "Seriously. You want to squeeze it?"

"I don't want to squeeze anything," she said dryly. He pumped the black bulb attached to the line and returned to the console, Roz following.

"You want to start it now?" he asked.

She shook her head, her hair shifting with the movement. "Fine. I admit it. I don't know what I'm doing, and apparently, you do. If you can start the stupid thing, start it." She crossed her arms again and watched him, and he took a second to enjoy the discomfiture in her eyes.

"My pleasure," Alden finally said. "You have to put it in neutral and push this forward." He moved the lever and turned the key. The engine started up, racing.

"Is it supposed to do that?" Roz asked with concern.

Alden popped the lever into place, and the engine purred. "Now we're idling. Want to release the transom line?"

"Transom?"

He laughed again. "The back. Did you seriously never ride on your dad's boat?"

"I did, but mostly I was reading or just enjoying the waves and sunbathing," she said as she released the rope and the boat shifted farther from the dock. "He and my mom were fishing and doing the boat things."

"The boat things." Alden smiled, imagining her in a bikini, a teenager without a care in the world, reclining idly in the sun with a book. He was probably doing the same thing at that age, only not in a bikini.

He pushed the lever forward, then found the battery switch and selected battery two. Always good policy to charge up the backup. He moved the boat slowly out into the small marina and toward the open water.

"How do you know about boats?" Roz asked.

"Our family had a lake house in upstate New York. Many pleasant summer vacations involved boats."

"Of course they did," she said. "Poor little rich boy?"

"You apparently grew up in paradise. Are you complaining?"

"No," she said, her voice softening. "Sorry. I'm just not used to asking for help. I'll try to keep my insults to things I actually know about."

Alden chuckled. "Fair enough. I'm sure I can count on your devotion to fact-checking."

As they eased into the lagoon and headed north toward the inlet, the marina lights receded behind them, and stars shone above. The moon had already set, so the night seemed incredibly black, except for the scant glow of their controls and navigation lights and the glint of houses on the near and far shores. This was so different from his previous life in South Florida, all noise and speed and glitter.

"Do you know where you're going?" she asked.

"Not exactly. Earl was going to get me there. He promised. Only Earl is a better drinking buddy than he is a fisherman, apparently. And you?"

"I have coordinates. GPS," Roz said. "This, I know how to do."

She moved closer to him at the console and keyed in the coordinates on the GPS unit. The colorful map on the display showed their route, with the time, direction, speed and current water depth—important in the mostly shallow lagoon. If he strayed from the channel, they could run aground.

Roz pointed to the screen, indicating a point out in the ocean. "That's about where it happened. We should be able to get a look just when the sun comes up, see what we can learn."

"Probably not much," Alden said. "But I figured it was worth a shot. If the explosion was so violent the boat was in small pieces, like your story said—"

"Aw, you read my story?" Her tone was sarcastic again.

"Of course." He didn't miss a beat. "Then it must have had a violent cause. Maybe it was just a gas leak—"

"That would do it?" she asked, moving closer to hear him over the motor. Even with the odor of fuel wafting around them, she smelled like jasmine, and he got distracted for a second.

"Sure," he said, clearing his throat, speaking more softly so she'd have to lean closer. "A spark would do it—if they had the wrong parts in the engine and fumes collected in the bilge, say."

"That doesn't seem like murder," Roz said.

"You sound disappointed. It could have been sabotage, though an accident is a lot more likely."

Roz gripped the console as they approached the inlet and Alden steered them in a wide curve to enter the passage. "What if there was something criminal happening?" she asked. "Maybe they were running drugs or something. Duke told me the Coast Guard was nearby when it happened. Maybe they were already investigating drug runners in the area. Or maybe that boat carried more than fish."

"Why would Boyd Bellamy want to run drugs? He's richer than Midas."

"The fishing guide might be another story. He might've needed money," Roz said, and then she shut up.

Alden raised an eyebrow at her. "So we need to look into his financials."

"There you go with that 'we' again," she said, but good-naturedly. "Yeah, that would probably be wise. See if he has a record and all that. That guy Verret said he was a fine young guide. Seemed pretty broken up about it."

"Of course. He lost a really expensive boat."

"That's pretty cynical." Roz looked into his eyes. They were still standing there in the dim glow of the console instead of retreating to the twin captain's chairs, and the motion of the boat in the waves of the inlet rocked them toward each other. It was all he could do to not to let himself fall against her.

"I'm a cynical guy," he admitted.

"That's too bad," Roz said, still holding his gaze.

Her tone seemed ... regretful. He had the oddest thought: He didn't want to disappoint her.

"Just looking at all the angles," he said as coolly as he could.

She shrugged and looked at the GPS as they passed under the causeway bridge and got closer to the ocean. She kept an eye on the digital map as he exited the inlet and entered the Atlantic. He opened up the engine and pushed them, bouncing, in the direction of the wreckage. It was hard to talk over the noise, so they didn't.

"Another mile," Roz called out after several minutes of roaring through the darkness. "You might want to slow down, keep an eye out for debris."

At that moment, there was a *thunk* as the bow of the boat struck something.

"Slow down! Slow down!" Roz waved her hands at him and moved toward the edge of the deck, scanning the water.

Alden pulled back on the throttle, slowing them to a crawl. "It wasn't that big, whatever it was. We're OK."

"Let me get a brighter light so we don't run into anything bigger." Roz moved to a side compartment and pulled out a handheld spotlight. She switched it on, and the brilliant beam cut a swath into the night, just as the slightest hint of gray touched the eastern horizon.

Roz swept the surface of the water with the beam, occasionally calling out to Alden to shift right or left.

"Is that port or starboard?" he teased on the third or fourth command.

"Shut up," she said. "Oh, look. There's more stuff in the water here. What does the GPS say?"

"We're just about on it," Alden said, looking at the display. "Maybe we should put down the anchor until the sun comes up."

"I think it's OK if we drift." She moved next to him, and before he could stop her, she turned the key. The engine died.

"Why did you do that?" His voice sounded more strident than he intended.

"So we can drift."

"Never turn off a boat offshore. Ever," he said. "You might not get it started again."

"Pshaw," she scoffed. "Don't tell me what to do. It's my boat. Isn't this nice? It's so quiet. And you can almost see the stars reflected in the water."

Alden shook his head, then put his annoyance aside. It was just boater's paranoia, he told himself. And with the engine off, it *was* nice—eerily peaceful in the near-darkness, away from all the pressures of the past, of expectations. And Roz's energy, as abrasive as it was, inexplicably lightened his heart.

She opened another compartment and pulled out a bag, and then a camera, before stuffing the bag back into the cubby. She handed him the spotlight. "I'm going to take a few photos."

As his eyes adjusted, the scant light of early, early morning began to lend the sky the sheen of a black pearl, and the water reflected the change. In it, he saw scattered, amorphous objects. She snapped several pictures under the light of the beam, but even with the spotlight, it was difficult to get an idea of what they were looking at. It didn't all seem like boat parts, but it was hard to tell. Some of the flotsam clunked gently against the hull.

At one point, his beam caught the glint of white fiberglass. "That has to be from the boat," he said.

Roz rummaged in her bag and mounted a big flash on the camera. She aimed toward the piece and shot a photo. The flash ripped open the semidarkness and blinded him for a second. Alden closed his eyes—and heard something.

He opened them again, turned off the spotlight and moved next to her. "Do you hear that?"

"What?" She shot off the camera again, the harsh white flash slicing open the expiring night.

"A boat, maybe," he said.

"It could be the searchers, though Duke told me they weren't going to start till eight. They were exhausted after yesterday."

"Did you date that guy?" Alden hated himself for asking.

"High school dates. A few ice cream cones. Hardly dating."

"Good," Alden said.

Roz laughed. "Jealous of a high school boyfriend? Or I should say, friend who was a boy."

"And still is, presumably. No, I'm not jealous." *Probably.* "I just don't like the idea of you being too chummy with your sources."

"Ah, of course," she said, popping the flash again.

An echo of the flash seemed to dance in his retina.

Or was that—?

"Is somebody else taking photos, too?" Roz asked in puzzlement, looking across the water.

Alden heard a *crack.*

And saw a dim outline of a boat, not far off.

And then a flash and another *crack,* and a *ping* and a spark on the railing—

He grabbed Roz. "They're shooting at us! Get down!"

# chapter
## nine

"WHAT ARE YOU TALKING ABOUT?" Roz struggled as Alden pushed her to the deck between the captain's chairs. She started to stand as another crack rent the air and something splashed in the waves next to the boat. She dropped to the deck again. "Crap!"

"Tell me about it." Alden went to the console.

"What are you doing?" Roz heard the anxious note in her voice.

"Making sure it's in neutral." He turned the key.

*Click click click.*

"No," he said. "Just no."

"What? Start the boat!"

"Trying." Alden's expression suddenly shifted from horror to inspiration. "The battery! It's the batteries."

He did something to a switch, turned the key, and the engine roared to life. Then he rammed the boat into gear and spun the wheel, turning it back toward shore.

Another flash-*crack* split the semidarkness as Roz's vessel leapt forward. The other boat seemed to be getting closer.

"Maybe it's a mistake? Mistaken identity? Duck hunting?" Roz called in disbelief from where she crouched on the deck as another shot whizzed over their heads. *OK, maybe not.*

"Ask me if we make it out of this alive," Alden said over the engine's roar. "And do you see any ducks?"

"Speaking of, you should duck or something," she called, not very helpfully, she realized.

"I'm trying to pilot this thing." But Alden dropped to a crouch, steering from as low a position as he could manage.

Roz looked behind them, straining to see the other boat. It was closer to shore, so it wasn't backlit by the dawn light creeping into the eastern sky. But that meant her boat was, making it even more of a target.

Her adrenaline spiked as she saw another flash and flinched. The bullet went wide. "It's following us!" Fear replaced denial. "Who would be shooting at us?"

"Maybe we interrupted your drug dealers."

"They're not my drug dealers!"

"Whatever." He looked grim. "Any ideas?"

"Run like hell?"

"Besides that."

*Zing. Crack!* A bullet struck the bimini above them.

Alden cursed and looked over his shoulder. "I think they're gaining on us. And it sounds like at least two types of gun. So there's probably at least two people on board."

"How do you know that?"

"Time on the range. I shoot a little. Or at least I used to."

"Two shooters is not good," she said, following his gaze. "Should we call the Coast Guard on the radio?"

"Unless they can teleport here, I don't think they can get to us before that boat does. I've got the engine laid flat out, but we're only going about thirty knots," he said. "And now it's getting lighter. They can see us better all the time."

"That's not good either."

"I know," he said darkly. "I guess we'll have to make a run for the inlet."

"Not ideal," Roz said. "We can't speed through the inlet. Even if we wanted to violate the limit, there will be other boaters by now. Unknown factors and obstacles. And we'll lose a high-speed chase anyway."

"They might stop shooting with more people around."

"Maybe. But what if they don't? Then we're trapped in the lagoon. We'll still have to stop at some point, and we're outgunned and out-boated." She chewed her lip. Another bullet whizzed overhead. Maybe she and Alden needed a more radical plan. "What if we jumped off?"

"What?" Alden looked at her in disbelief. "Are you nuts?"

The wind rushing past them and the bouncing of the boat helped her understand his hesitation.

"We'll keep the boat running as a decoy," Roz said. "Get it up to top speed and let it go."

"We're already at top speed. Go on."

"Right. Well, first we have to get close enough to land so that we can swim ashore. Then we'll jump. It's still not totally light out. If we're lucky, they won't see us jump. They'll follow the boat."

Looking worried and strong and weirdly handsome in the moment before they were about to die, Alden glanced at their pursuers—*zing* went another bullet overhead—and then the console.

"I suppose I've heard worse ideas. Like that time the *Eye* wanted me to interview one of those man-eating white tigers in Vegas."

"You can't interview a tiger."

"Not for long, anyway."

She lifted her head a little and looked at the GPS, made a quick estimate. "In about three minutes we should be approaching the inlet. Parallel with it, anyway. You can swim, right?"

"Summers at the lake, remember?"

"Good. So when we're just off Stargazer Point, we make sure the boat is aimed south so it'll go for a while without running into something, and then we jump."

"Off the gunwale on the starboard side, so you don't get run over," Alden ordered.

"I'm not that dumb," Roz snapped.

Alden spun the wheel a bit to take their boat closer to shore, and Roz poked her head up to get a better look at their pursuers. They had a bigger vessel, but Roz couldn't see much more, even as it crept closer.

A bullet hit the top of the captain's chair she was clutching.

She gasped and ducked again. "That would have been my head!"

"But it wasn't." Alden reached for her and grabbed her hand, still driving with the other. "We'll be OK."

The feel of his warm hand on hers centered her, making her forget their bickering. She thought about getting back to Comet Cove, to her job, to her mom. This had to work.

"Should we get the life jackets?" she asked.

"Bright orange is probably not the best fashion choice in this situation," he said.

"You have a point." More *cracks,* more whizzing bullets. A couple of shots banged into the side of the boat. "Son of a—"

The gunfire sounded louder now. The mystery boat kept gaining, and their stalkers' aim was improving.

*They're not just trying to scare us off,* she thought. *They're trying to kill us.*

"Ready?" Alden asked.

Roz risked a glance at the GPS unit. The map showed their boat was almost parallel with the inlet—though still unnervingly far from shore. She looked into Alden's eyes, those lucid gray eyes that reflected the earliest blush of dawn, and nodded. "Ready."

Alden reached up and spun the wheel slightly to make the boat's direction more southerly. "Wide-open throttle," he said to himself as he touched the controls. Crawling, he tugged her toward the right side of the boat.

*Starboard,* she thought. *The right side. The right choice?* She hoped so. She never dreamed she'd be in this situation, especially with Alden. *Any port in a storm, right?*

Her brain was full of nonsense, her body full of adrenaline.

Roz realized she still had the camera in her hand. She turned off the flash, cranked up the ISO, lifted the Nikon and quickly took one snapshot in the direction of the pursuing boat, which still seemed cloaked in shadows. She popped out the memory card and stuck it in her shorts pocket, tucked the camera into a storage bench, then joined Alden at the rail. She slipped off her sweater and dropped it on the deck. She was chilly in her tank top, but at least it wouldn't drag her down. "Let's do it."

"Keep your head down as best you can and make toward shore, just over there. See it?"

"Yes." The point at Comet Cove, home of Lunaria Lodge, was a dim smudge on the sliding horizon, but the lighthouse flashed at intervals. They were already moving past it. Roz looked at Alden, took in the worry lines in his brow, the hard set to his jaw, and gave his hand a squeeze. She had another rapid, idle thought: She wanted to do that again. "See you there."

He managed a smile. "You bet."

She stepped up to the gunwale and dove overboard into the wide, dark, breath-snatching water.

chapter
# **ten**

ALDEN WATCHED her vanish beneath the waves and, after a moment's glance at their pursuers, dove in right behind her. He swam under the water for as long as he could, in the cold black universe of the Atlantic, seeing nothing, only hoping—hoping their loopy improvisation would work.

He broke the surface, fighting the waves, and gasped for air, looking around for Roz, trying to get oriented. At first, he didn't see anything, but then he spun and watched their boat rapidly leaving them.

With the other boat apparently still in pursuit.

He hoped Roz's boat would gain enough distance to crash into land far, far away from him and Roz but before the other crew—who the hell was it?—caught up to it. If the chasers did catch it and didn't find anyone on board, they might come looking. Even if the shooters didn't necessarily know who to look for.

A band of orange began to seep into the dark blues and purples of the predawn sky, all that old black and gray now giving in to a simmering cauldron of tropical Florida color.

Soon it would be easy to spot a couple of dark-headed people swimming toward shore in the sapphire sea.

Alden dared not call out for Roz, not yet, fearful of his voice carrying over the water. She had to be swimming, too. She was probably ahead of him, especially now that his wet jeans and shirt seemed to claw at him, dragging him down. He fought the feeling, kicked and swam, heading for the lumpy coastline of south Comet Cove.

He guessed they'd jumped a mile or so from shore, but a mile was a long way when the water was seventy degrees and they were tired and wearing heavy clothes and scared witless. A few times he thought he saw a head bobbing in the water in front of him, and a couple of dolphins broke the waves far ahead, near shore. Catching their breakfast, maybe.

He suddenly wanted coffee and pancakes. And to make sure Roz was OK.

He swam harder, drawing on all the hours he spent swimming at the gym, focusing on the rhythm, the breathing, trying to ignore his cramping muscles and heavy clothes. When he looked up again, he was a lot closer to shore, and he could make out a figure in the water ahead of him, not moving.

"Roz!" he called out in concern, then looked around. The other boat was out of sight. Relief mixed with trepidation as he swam harder, trying to reach her. A swift shape ruffled the water next to him, and he glimpsed a dolphin swimming alongside him. The moment was surreal, comforting. He looked ahead again. The figure he'd seen was definitely Roz.

She lay back, floating, only her face above the water, her eyes closed. They fluttered open when he touched her. "Just resting," she croaked, then bobbed forward on a wave, gripping his shoulder. Her hand was like ice.

He did his best to tread water for both of them. "We're almost there. Can you do it?"

"I think so."

"I'll help you."

She started swimming, a mix of breaststroke and a slow crawl, and he swam alongside her, encouraging her.

The dolphin—no, dolphins, two of them—swept through the waves next to them, circled away and came back. Unformed tears filled Alden's eyes, a strange, warm sensation. He couldn't remember the last time he'd cried. Surely he wasn't now.

It was just the shock, he told himself. To Roz, he said, "The dolphins want us to make it."

Something shifted in her body, a new energy, and her pace increased.

"That's my girl," he said, trying to talk his own muscles into finishing the journey.

They fought the breaking waves near shore. Finally, when their feet found ground, it was on an undeveloped piece of beach lined with a thicket of mangroves. He put an arm around Roz's waist and walked her along the shore until he found a more secluded spot, a miniature bay where a stream trickled toward the sea. He tugged her arm, trying to get her into the shelter of the bushes.

Her face was deathly pale. "Stop here," she mumbled.

"We should get out of sight," Alden said, but she wavered and plopped down on the sand, breathing hard, in a daze. "This isn't going to work," he murmured. "Let me help you."

He reached down and scooped her up.

"Urrmm," was all she said, her head lolling back against his shoulder.

It might have been an objection. It might have been an

incoherent thought. But he had to get them out of sight, and she was exhausted. She was a solid bundle in his arms, not as warm as she should have been, but still, heat ignited under his chilled skin as he held her close.

Alden picked his way behind a wall of scrubby bushes that should hide them from wayward killers and gently set her down. She flopped back against the sand with a groan. He sat hard next to her and slowly unbuttoned his sodden flannel shirt, dropping it to the ground, hoping the now rising sun would warm him, dry his T-shirt. For a while, he just leaned forward against his knees, breathing hard. And then he turned to her.

"Are you OK?"

"Not dead, so that's good," she said, her eyes still closed.

Alden laughed, a laugh of pure relief. "At least we agree on something." He laid a hand on her arm. "You're shivering."

"No sh—sh—"

"Still the smart-ass." He lay on his side next to her and wrapped an arm around her. "Shhh," he said to her murmured protest, moving closer so his body pressed against hers. "We need to warm up."

"OK," was all she said, and after a moment, she snuggled closer to him. He wrapped his arms around her, and they slowly warmed with the sun and the heat of their bodies.

God, she felt good. And even after their ordeal, the swim through the chilly waters, he could have sworn her skin gave off a hint of jasmine. Alden pushed his nose into her neck and nuzzled her.

She shifted against him. "Mmmm." Was she asleep?

He was feeling better. Or at least part of him was, pushed up against her. He was afraid to move.

Instead, he kissed her neck.

The salty taste of her went right to his head. And still Roz lay there, as if in a dream, sleeping beauty, her chestnut hair in damp clumps around her face and shoulders.

Alden slipped a hand under her wet tank top, laying it lightly on her belly, and kissed her neck again. This time he lingered, tonguing the skin as she stretched languorously against him.

He trailed kisses along her jaw, giving in to his craving as every rational cell in his brain screamed at him not to. He hesitated only a moment, taking in the soft angles of her face, her closed eyes fringed with dark lashes, her skin dusted with sparkles of sand. And then he touched his lips to hers, tasting her, salty and sweet. She lifted one of her arms; was she pushing him away?

Electricity shot through him as she slipped her fingers into his hair and pulled him closer.

Surprised, he opened his mouth over hers, sliding his tongue between her lips, and she responded, moaning softly. He clutched her waist more tightly as he kissed her. Around them, the water whispered, the breeze rustled the bushes, and the birds chirped soft calls of encouragement. An ache grew inside him as he pulled her closer, as the interplay of lips and tongues grew more heated, promising more, so much more.

And then she froze.

And pushed him off.

"Alden," she said, half-dazed, half-scolding, opening her eyes.

"Roz," he said gruffly, the pressure of desire chasing away any remnants of cold.

"We shouldn't," she whispered, and she struggled to sit up.

He helped her, reluctant to stop touching her. "Do you feel better?"

Roz looked into his eyes, and her hazel gaze seared him. It seemed so vulnerable, so full of light.

Light. Yes, there was a lot more light now.

She blinked. "We need to get back to civilization. Any sign of our boat? Or that other one?"

He sighed. The dream was over. "No boats."

"We might want a boat if we're where I think we are."

"Which is where?" he asked.

"I think we're on the beach of the wildlife preserve south of the resort."

"Maybe it's a desert island and we'll have to live off coconuts until someone finds us."

"Ha." Roz got to her feet, which were still clad in her frayed tennis shoes, and dusted the sand off her legs. "Not if our GPS was working."

"That explains why we're the only people on the beach." Willing his longing to cool, Alden stood and tied his still-damp flannel shirt around his waist. He'd lost his boat shoes somewhere in the ocean—and, he realized after a panicked pat of his pockets, his phone—but he'd have to walk anyway. There was nowhere to go but back into the heart of Comet Cove.

"Show me the way," he said.

# eleven

THE DESIGNATED wilderness area along the beach stretched all the way to A1A, acres and acres of scrub and swamp and mangrove islets with a shallow lake at its heart. It used to be owned by one of the town's oldest dynasties, the somewhat mysterious Esquivel family—the same one that sold the Lunaria Lodge property to the Reyes family for development five years earlier. A year ago, the Esquivels donated the wild area to Comet Cove, with the stipulation it should be preserved as naturally as possible. The town was still working on making it accessible to visitors. Which meant no trails or signs.

The best way through a watery thicket like this was a kayak, Roz thought after the first twenty minutes of trying to find a passage through it. The branches viciously scratched at them, the insects bit, and goodness knows what was waiting for them in the water. Eventually, as the sun rose, they found a small, winding channel—a shaded mangrove tunnel—they could wade through. She hoped it was taking them farther west. She was arguing with Alden about directions when he almost walked right into a snake dangling from an overhanging branch.

"You're lucky it's just a water snake," Roz said after he cursed the near-collision.

"Lucky?" He sounded skeptical.

"Could've been a cottonmouth. They both bite, but a cottonmouth'll kill you. Watch your toes."

"Great," he said, and she chuckled. She hated to admit it, but a small part of her was actually enjoying this miserable outing.

After almost an hour of slogging back and forth and crossing their own path, then having to navigate around the lake, they finally found an area that looked different. The landscape here had fewer mangroves and more palmettos, adorned with sharp-edged fronds. Roz and Alden found a narrow, dry path carved by some other explorer, slightly overgrown but better than wading in the chilly water. The landscape transitioned to a tropical hammock, with live oaks, cabbage palms, the purple blooms of morning glory, and other scrubby plants Roz couldn't identify.

And then, finally, Roz spotted an unlikely swath of emerald green through the trees ahead of them.

"What is that, a golf course?" Alden asked, sounding tired.

Roz trotted ahead, grateful for her sneakers, and paused at the tree line.

"Actually, yes," she said.

Alden appeared next to her. They both stepped out onto the grass, into the open, and Roz paused to relish the feel of the unimpeded sun soaking into her tired, cold, damp body. But then she hesitated and looked around with a rush of nerves, reliving their close call this morning, when someone was trying to kill her. Them. Could someone be waiting for them? Someone with a gun?

*Don't be silly. The bad guys were on a boat, and they don't know who you are.*

"Roz?" Alden asked. "You OK?"

She got ahold of herself. "Yes. Let's go." They set out across the springy, groomed grass.

In the distance was the golf club, under construction—midway through its expansion—set among a pleasing landscape of manicured lawn, ponds, and islands of palms and flowering plants.

"So this is where our sports reporter spends all his time," Alden said. "And they aren't even finished yet."

"Yeah, but there's a lot of stuff going on. A big tournament is coming here soon, I hear. Not that that's my beat," she added.

"What is your beat?"

"Everything except sports. Plus editing. Crap, I have to get to the office and wrap up this week's edition."

"One thing at a time," Alden said. "Don't you need to get to your car first?"

"What about you?" she asked as they set off across the lawn toward the clubhouse.

"I biked to the wharf. If we can get there, I can bicycle home."

"Don't be silly," Roz said. "I'll give you and your bike a ride."

"I'd like you to give me a ride."

She caught his impish tone and shot a look at him. He was grinning.

"I thought you were too tired to be incorrigible," she said.

"Do you really mind? God, this grass feels good on my feet."

Roz looked down and gasped. "Oh my God, Alden." His feet were covered in scratches and cuts from their sojourn through the scrub.

"I'll be OK. Next time I'm wearing flippers."

"There better not be a next time," she said.

"You may get your wish, since you no longer have a boat."

"I hope it doesn't run into anything important or kill someone."

"It'll probably run out of gas first," Alden said. "The next question is, how are we going to report this?"

"You mean in the paper? I'm inclined not to report anything until we figure out what it was. But, I mean, I can't control what you print."

"I'm actually wondering if we should report our little encounter to the cops. But if we do, it becomes public record, and I'm not sure I'm ready for that," Alden said. "I don't want to look like an idiot in my own paper or anyone else's. I need to know a lot more before we run a headline that says, 'Reporter shot at by unknown goons while riding on rival reporter's boat.'"

"I thought you said you wanted me to give you a ride?" Roz teased, unable to help herself.

"That's different." Alden grinned again. He put a warm hand on her shoulder as they neared a cluster of structures, some still under construction. "Hey, do you think the bar's open?"

"What?" Roz looked up at the buildings. "Ha. Actually, no. Looks like it'll be huge when it's done, though. Maybe we can find someone to help us."

They rounded the outdoor bar in the final stages of

construction and spotted a couple of guys on ladders, painting, as the echoing sound of hammering emitted from inside the building. Roz couldn't help but be impressed, even if her reporting showed the updated course would be a water guzzler the city could ill afford.

One of the painters noticed them and ambled over to where they were standing. The paint-spattered young man, with a deep tan and sandy hair, looked them over suspiciously. "Can I help you?"

"We had a boating accident," Alden said smoothly. "We had to walk quite a way. Could someone call us a cab or a rideshare? Neither of us have phones."

*And at least I left mine with my wallet in my car,* Roz thought. She wondered about Alden's. She'd already lost her camera and other sundries, but her keys were still in her pocket. It could be worse.

"You two look like you've had quite a morning," the painter said. "I'm about to go grab lunch for the guys. I can take you somewhere, as long as it's in Comet Cove."

"That would be wonderful. I'm Roz, and this is Alden."

"Rick," said the painter, flashing a winning smile, reaching out to shake their hands. "Give me five minutes."

"Thank God," Roz whispered as the painter went off to touch base with his buddies.

Alden rubbed her back again. She didn't pull away. She tried to tell herself it was because she was still chilly and he was so warm. She was starting to like him touching her, but any contact between them was not a good idea. She had a paper to save. She needed her independence. She needed her own scoops. And she didn't need ...

"It'll be OK," Alden murmured into her hair, so close it

almost felt like a kiss, and her every rational thought took flight.

Twenty-five minutes later, painter Rick dropped Roz and Alden off at Southside Wharf. It was after eleven, according to Alden's adventure watch, and there was more activity than earlier, with fishermen and pleasure boaters coming and going. Still, it was a lot quieter than Star Harbor on the north side of the inlet, and maybe that was a good thing, he thought.

"You go on. I can bike home," Alden said to Roz. "But we should probably talk at some point about what happened this morning. The gunfire, I mean."

Was it his imagination, or did she blush? "I told you I'd give you a ride," she said. "Otherwise the pedals are going to rip up your poor feet even more."

"I'm not sure my bike will fit in your car."

"Oh, sure it will," she said, leading him to the hybrid. She pulled her keys out of her pocket and pressed the button on her fob. Nothing happened. She pressed again. "What the—?"

"Salt water is the worst," said Alden. "It's a miracle you still have keys at all."

Roz rolled her eyes and pressed a button on the side of the fob, releasing a small key. With some wrangling of seats, they stuffed his bicycle in the back, then climbed into the front.

Roz pushed the ignition button. Nothing happened. She rubbed her temples.

"Headache?" Alden asked.

"Trying to remember how to push-button start with a dead fob."

"Here." He plucked the fob from her hand and pressed it against the button until he heard a soft beep. "Now press it."

She looked at him, then pressed the button. The car started. "Are you the engine whisperer or something?"

"I like to read about cars. It helps me relax. If I really want to relax, a good car manual helps put me to sleep."

"Exciting reading," Roz said, putting the hybrid in gear and taking them out of the lot. She wended through the neighborhoods and back to Highway A1A.

Alden had so much trouble sleeping, even car manuals were too exciting sometimes, but she didn't need to know that. "I also read novels, but I have to be careful, or they'll keep me awake all night. I have trouble putting them down."

"Really?" she asked, heading north. "What do you read?"

"Thrillers. So-called literary stuff. The occasional sci-fi. And I keep saying I'm going to write a novel someday."

"I once had an editor who told me every journalist has a novel manuscript in their bottom drawer," Roz said.

Alden smiled. "I wish. Mine's not written yet. What do you like to read?"

Her smile was bashful. "I read widely, but I'm afraid I bask in guilty pleasures."

His imagination went right to the guiltiest pleasures he could imagine. "What guilty pleasures?"

"So where do you live?" she asked, changing the subject.

"Oh, yeah." Alden directed her through south Comet Cove and its more modest neighborhoods, to his street and a yellow, two-story stucco house. Oak trees shaded its front yard, with palms and bougainvillea adding color and motion. "I'm the second-floor apartment."

"Nice balcony." Roz peered out the window as she parked.

Plants lined the railing, the work of his landlady. "Uh, do you have your keys?"

"I hide one under the clay frog in the plant by the door. In case you ever need it." He shot her a flirtatious smile.

They wrestled his bike from the back, and then it was time to part. Only Alden didn't want to. He struggled for something to say after the intensity of the morning, remembering her leap overboard, the fear, the feel of her lips against his.

She held his gaze for a moment and nodded, almost as if agreeing with his unspoken thoughts, then got into her car.

"Remember to call me about the carriage people," he said before she could close the door. "But give me an hour or two to get a new phone."

"Oh, crap, I'm sorry."

"It's OK. I'll expense it. And then we can look into our gunboat."

Roz eyed him for a few seconds. "Too many loose ends," she said, brisk and businesslike again. "I'll call you later."

Alden watched her drive off, then hauled his bicycle up the outdoor staircase to his place, thinking about one loose end that was all too likely to entangle him: Roz Melander.

ROZ TOOK A LONG, hot shower at home, wondering if she should be taking a cold one. She had a lot to think about—a story from hell, almost getting killed, and losing her family's boat. And Alden.

She touched her lips as the hot water streamed over her, washing off the salt and cleaning the abrasions their jungle adventure had left on her skin. He'd kissed her, and she'd kissed him back, and it had been amazing. But it would have to end there. It had to.

She knew that saving the *Courier* from ruin was more important than her own foolish desires. But she still thought about him, how he'd pressed against her, how tender and warm his lips had been on hers, and she ached for him, ached for everything she'd been missing in life.

She cranked the temperature all the way to cold and, a minute later, got out of the shower, shivering. She dressed quickly, in jeans and a black knit shirt with three-quarter sleeves, good enough for casual Florida. She needed comfort, even as she needed to work fast.

Roz rinsed her camera's memory card and set it out to dry,

hoping the gadget's famed durability held up to a thorough soaking in salt water. While she nuked spaghetti left over from one of her rare nights of cooking, she thought about what had happened on the boat.

The first question on her mind: Who had shot at them? The second, inextricably linked with the first: Why?

Maybe they had interrupted a drug deal, but they'd barely spotted the other boat when the gunfire started. And didn't a drug deal involve more than one boat? No other vessels had been in sight. And why stage a deal there, right where the fishing boat had exploded, just as the sun was coming up? It made no sense.

The third question, which she pondered over her pasta: Did the shooters have any idea who she and Alden were? She thought not. But they seemed willing to kill. Reporting the incident to the police right away—which would make her and Alden's identity public record—seemed like a bad idea for now. If and when her boat was found, the truth might come out. She never liked lying, even by omission, but something told her caution was in order.

At the least, she could get the latest on the Bellamy accident and recovery efforts. She tried Duke first.

"Hi, Roz," he said after the department patched her through to the deputy. "What can I do for you?"

"Just wondering how the search was going."

"We're going to release it later today, but we found—uh— evidence that there were no survivors," he said with a level of discomfort she found amusing in a law enforcement officer.

"Remains?"

"That's a good word for it."

Roz swallowed, trying not to picture it. "Have you learned what happened to the boat?"

"I think the Coast Guard is looking into it, but they're pretty busy with other interdictions at the moment. My guess is it's going to come down to some kind of hardware failure."

"Gas leak?" Roz asked, remembering Alden's comments this morning.

"Could be. Look, can you wait an hour before you publish about the victims? That's when the release is coming out. It'll look bad for me if too much leaks out in advance."

"Not a problem," she said, thinking Alden would never agree. But this was a source she didn't want to burn. "Thanks for giving me a head start."

"Maybe I'll see you at the Milky Way," Duke teased.

"Why don't you give me your cell?" she asked, hoping he wouldn't take her question the wrong way. She wanted a direct line to her source, not a date. He cheerfully gave her the number, and they said their goodbyes.

She had enough for a story, for sure—the confirmed death of Boyd Bellamy, not to mention his trusty fishing guide. Who, she reminded herself, should be checked out as well.

She called Consummate Catch next and, to her pleasant surprise, was put through to the president.

"Mr. Verret, it's Roz Melander from the *Comet Cove Courier*. I just wanted to say how sorry I am for the loss of your fishing guide."

"How nice of you," Verret said, his tone as dry as Death Valley. "And?"

Roz plowed on. "I wondered if you had any more clues as to why the boat might have exploded?"

"Consummate Catch is investigating the possibility of an accident caused by a fuel leak, and we are cooperating fully with the authorities. We truly regret the loss of life and want to reassure the public and our customers that our boats are rigorously maintained. Our entire fleet will be undergoing a thorough safety check."

"Is that what the press release says?" Roz asked.

Verret's tone shifted from robotic to snarky. "Which you would have known if you'd looked at our website."

"I prefer to go to the source, sir," she said, but she scrambled on her laptop to pull up the release. It contained no names; actually, no reference to victims at all. Selective truth. "We'd like to write a nice obituary for your guide. Do you mind sharing his name?"

Verret paused, and then he gave her the name, which she typed into her file. She also got out of him that the guide was single and a nice guy who knew some of the best fishing spots in central Florida.

"So do a lot of people fish where the boat exploded?" she asked.

"No," Verret said. "That was a spot our guides knew about, but we didn't advertise it."

"So none of your boats would have been out there, say, early this morning?"

Verret paused again. He paused a lot. She wondered what he was thinking. "Why would you ask?"

Roz wasn't ready to tell him she and Alden had been pursued by crazed gunmen. "Just—something I heard about a boat at the accident scene. Or boats."

"Our search resumed at eight this morning. Perhaps that's what you saw?"

"No, that wasn't—no, that's not what I heard," Roz said, recovering herself. Who was interviewing who here? "Thanks for your help, and again, I'm sorry for your loss."

"I hope we can all put this behind us," he said coolly. "Goodbye, Ms. Melander."

Verret was irritating, Roz thought, but at least she'd learned the name of the guide. A quick search turned up no criminal record on that poor young man, at least.

Time to look into other angles, even if they were more Alden's style than hers. She'd promised.

She dialed Pegasus Stables, whose services included carriage rides. The woman who answered the phone hooked her up with the owner, April Reins. Talk about naming being destiny.

"Liani mentioned the carriage ride?" April replied to Roz's query. "There's not much more to tell you. We respect the privacy of anyone who hires us, particularly our guests from Lunaria Lodge, but truth be told, I have no idea who Boyd wanted to bring with him."

"He had plans for a guest?"

"Yes. It's kind of sad, isn't it? One day you're planning a romantic trip in a horse carriage through our quaint downtown, and then—you just disappear."

"But you think it was romantic?"

"That I can't say for sure," April said, "but what's more romantic than a horse-drawn carriage?"

Depends on your sense of smell, Roz thought. "And I suppose Liani won't share upcoming or canceled room reservations," she mused.

"I think we both know the answer to that, but you can ask. Not my circus, not my monkeys."

Roz chuckled. "You're the expert on circuses." April used to perform in one. Roz had seen pictures of her in her sequined cowgirl outfit standing on top of two horses at once, a foot on each horse's back, grinning in the spotlight as her reddish-blond hair streamed out behind her. "Listen, I think you've told me all I need to know, but there's this other reporter who wants to talk to you —"

"Who would that be?"

"Alden Knox. He's—"

"That cutie at *The Beacon*? You want me to be unavailable?" April laughed.

Women all over town had noticed Alden, Roz thought, and the notion was curiously annoying. "No, just, uh, giving you a heads-up that he might call."

"No problem. We have nothing to hide here! Especially since we seem to know less than you do."

Roz smiled at the painful truth. "Thanks, April. Have a good one."

"Take care, Roz."

Roz checked the starburst clock in her retro kitchen—one of the few pieces she'd kept when she sold off or donated most of her stuff to move into this furnished rental—and cursed under her breath. That press release would be out any minute. She wrote up a quick story with the information about the victims and the likely cause of the explosion, leaving out the bit about the carriage ride, and put it in the staging area on the *Courier*'s website. She checked her account for the sheriff's department's email and let it simmer for a couple of minutes until the press release appeared in her inbox, then hit the publish button on her story.

### *BOYD BELLAMY CONFIRMED DEAD IN BOAT EXPLOSION*

... That's what her site's headline said.

She switched over to *The Beacon*. There was no new story.

Five minutes later, there was, but with less information than hers and no byline. Maybe Alden was still working on replacing his phone. She felt gleeful—and possibly a bit guilty, which was ridiculous, because no matter what had happened this morning, she and Alden were still competing for the biggest story Comet Cove had seen in years. And the *Courier*'s web traffic already showed a big bump that should translate into more advertising, more dollars and a chance to sell the newspaper and get out.

She felt a stab of guilt about that, too. Her mother wanted to shed the business, but Roz getting out also meant leaving Mom here alone in Comet Cove.

Maybe, after one more phone call, Roz could spare a few minutes for a quick visit before she went back to the office. And maybe she could get her mom's insight into the story—and her conflicted hormones—without actually confessing anything.

chapter
## thirteen

ALDEN WALKED up the stairs to his office at *The Beacon* on tender feet, cushioned by gauze, socks and cross-trainers, though the wounds weren't all that bad after he'd cleaned them up and coated them in antibiotic ointment. Only a few scratches were deep enough to cause him real discomfort; his biggest concern was some nasty tropical swamp germ taking hold and turning him into a zombie.

But now, refreshed and clean in khakis and a pale blue button-up shirt, with a burrito from Taco Titan in his belly, he felt a lot better—even if Roz had scooped him while he was driving back from his visit to the phone store. One of his colleagues had slapped a story online, and he'd made a few phone calls from the road, but now it was time to dig in and get something fresh.

His new phone rang in his pocket. He answered it as he sat down. "Alden Knox."

"It's Roz."

"That's funny. I was just thinking that I never gave you my cell number. Shows what a good reporter you are."

"It was on your office voicemail."

"Then scooping me on the latest story shows what a good reporter you are."

"Maybe I had an unfair advantage," she said, her tone warming slightly.

"All's fair in love and war, especially now that I have my cell phone back. I saw you talked to the fishing company. They wouldn't give me the time of day. Anything you want to tell me?"

"I'll only tell you this because you deserve to know—Verret said he didn't have any boats in the area this morning before search and rescue resumed."

"Hmm," Alden replied. "Did you tell him we were there?"

"I told him I'd heard a report of a boat in the area."

"If it was one of his boats, he's probably wondering how you knew about it."

"Why would he have a boat in the area? Especially one with guns?" Roz asked.

"I don't know, but if he shot at us, he wouldn't tell us."

She harrumphed. "You're being paranoid."

"Almost as if someone nearly shot me to death at dawn."

"Oh, that," Roz said dismissively, and he laughed. "Listen, I called April Reins about the carriage ride. She owns Pegasus Stables."

"Pegasus like the winged horse?" That name was funny enough, but April Reins?

"More like Pegasus the constellation, modeled on the winged horse," Roz corrected him. "Anyway, she said she didn't know any more than what Liani told me, except that Boyd Bellamy was supposed to have a guest. Who, she didn't know. I let it go at that."

"Did you set up an interview?"

"I'm telling you now what she said."

"But I want to talk to her," Alden replied.

"Then freakin' call her and talk to her." Roz sounded exasperated. "I have a print deadline to meet this afternoon, and I don't have time to re-interview someone for no reason."

"Perhaps I will."

"OK."

There was silence on the other end for a moment, and Alden couldn't help filling the gap. "Want to do dinner and talk about our date with death?"

"It wasn't a date, and we didn't die, and I'm seriously on deadline, Alden," Roz said more kindly. "I promise if I learn anything directly related to the gunners or my boat, I'll let you know."

"Ah, I see. Duty calls."

"I'll—I'll talk to you later." Did he hear regret in her voice?

"I look forward to it," Alden said, and they rang off.

Just as well. She was the competition, for Christ's sake.

He wandered into John's office. His editor was mumbling over a story he was slashing and burning, if the on-screen changes were any indication.

"Got a minute?" Alden asked.

"Urrrrgh." John spun on his chair to face Alden, chewing hard on his gum, his blue eyes sparking with frustration.

"Thought you might want an update on the Bellamy story."

"Better late than never," John said significantly, his bushy eyebrows almost comical, his gray-streaked black hair a jumbled mess. He made it stick up even more by pushing his glasses up on his head as he leaned back to listen.

"I'll make it up to you," Alden said. "She only beat us by five minutes."

"And at least five inches."

"Ouch."

John waved at the one empty chair. "Sit down."

Alden sat, feeling surrounded. The other two chairs were piled high with newspapers. The file cabinets and John's desk were cluttered with papers, magazines, press releases, folders, empty coffee cups, and a couple of photos of his wife and twin girls at Disney World. Between two overflowing pen holders, a figurine of a lion mascot wearing an Orlando City soccer uniform bobbled its head as if it were listening.

"I had an unusual morning," Alden said.

"So I gathered when you called me to say you'd be late when you were already three hours late."

"I went to the accident site to check it out."

"How?"

"By boat, of course."

John's eyebrows met in the middle. "Whose boat?"

"Therein lies the rub. I happened upon Roz Melander when I went down to Southside Wharf, and since my ride bailed, I talked her into taking me with her."

"That sounds cozy," John said, with just a hint of a smile.

"Somebody shot at us."

John's eyebrows shot up as he rocked forward in his chair. "You OK?"

"We're both OK, though Roz's boat may be on its way to the Bahamas, and I got an intimate tour of the wilds of south Comet Cove."

"What happened?"

Alden gave him the short version, and John looked thoughtful.

"I don't want you taking any fool risks. It might have been drug dealers or worse," John said.

"We thought of that, but why there? Why right where the accident happened?"

"Maybe they blew up the fishing boat, too."

"And returned to the scene of the crime? It doesn't make sense."

John shook his head. "Strange. Keep an eye on it. And be careful. Don't go out there again on your own."

"That's an easy promise to make. I never want to repeat that experience." *Except for maybe that slow, salty kiss.*

"You got leads? I want something juicy on Bellamy. What he was doing here. Something that will get people interested. They don't really care about explosions unless they're on video."

"Exactly my point to Ms. Melander."

"And don't fraternize with the competition, unless you can use it to your advantage."

Alden smirked as if he found the very idea amusing, but privately, he eagerly imagined what fraternizing might involve. "I'm heading back to Lunaria Lodge this afternoon after I try to talk to the people who were giving Bellamy a carriage ride."

"As long as you're not horsing around." John grinned as he waited for Alden's groan. "Get out of here. And don't expense another dinner at Sirenia. We can't afford your taste in wine."

"Yes, sir." Alden smiled and left the office, pausing for a moment as he sat in his car to program the address of Pegasus Stables into his phone. The map showed it just south of Lighthouse Road on the way to Lunaria Lodge. Perfect.

The drive was pleasant, especially up Lighthouse Road, this time with the top down. He really liked the tropical foliage when he didn't have to hack his way through it in bare feet.

He made the right turn on a road that hadn't been paved in a while, drove past an older subdivision and found himself in a more open area among businesses that required more space—a plant nursery, an RV storage lot, and the stables.

He parked in the gravel lot and eyed the green pastures, dotted with deciduous trees and tall pines. White fences surrounded the fields. A wide, low gray barn was trimmed in white, clean and modern-looking. He got out of the car and walked past the open barn door. Inside, stalls flanked a roomy center aisle.

Before he could even get to the door marked "Office," a fortysomething woman emerged. She had long, strawberry-blond hair and a deep tan and wore jeans, a T-shirt and cowboy boots. The diamond studs in her ears caught the light.

"Roz told me you'd be in touch," she said.

"Oh, did she?" Alden wondered if Roz was looking out for him or warning off his sources. "So you know who I am?"

"I sure do. And I'm April Reins."

"Do you bring May flowers?"

"You're a funny one, aren't you? Cute, too." She grinned again. "What can I do for you? I told Roz what I knew, which wasn't much."

Alden joined her in strolling toward the fence that bordered the nearest pasture, where a few horses nibbled on the grass.

"Boyd Bellamy booked a carriage ride with you, right?" he asked. "Would you have ridden out of here?"

"Not usually," she said. "We can do rides from here or around the resort—we're conveniently located for that—but mostly people want to ride horses, not carriages. I have a truck that can transport the whole kit, but I usually store the carriage in a garage I rent downtown. Then I just trailer a horse over. It's convenient for festivals and weekends during the season." The season meant the cooler months. Nicer for the horses. "Boyd Bellamy wanted to ride around downtown."

Alden leaned against the fence. "And he had a guest?"

"He said he would bring a guest. He didn't tell me who."

"What do people do on these carriage rides? I mean besides just sit there."

"Some do that." April sounded amused. "Mostly they enjoy the view, take pictures, get smoochy when it's romantic. Propose when it's really romantic. Drink champagne."

"Do they eat, too?"

"A picnic isn't unusual," she said. "Especially since I plan stops according to the client's wishes, like at Boardwalk Park on the north side of the inlet. That's a beautiful place for a picnic or to grab ice cream and fries at the Milky Way."

"Do you source the picnic?"

"I can, but usually I make recommendations. If someone is staying at the resort, I recommend the restaurant there. Sirenia even has a picnic menu. It's really swank."

"Is that what Boyd Bellamy planned?" Alden asked.

"He did ask about food, and I recommended Sirenia and stopping at the park. That was the last I heard from him."

"Poor guy."

"I know. You gotta live for today, don't you?" April gave him a sly look. "Let me know if you want to ride around downtown sometime."

"That's kind of you." He smiled. He liked her direct approach, but he had other interests at the moment. "Thanks. I appreciate your time."

"Glad to help, if I helped. Tell Roz I said hi." Now she looked mischievous as she waved and walked back to the office.

Maybe he didn't get many details, but April had given him food for thought.

*Hmm. Food.*

He drove up to Lunaria Lodge and parked, then walked

around to where he thought the back door of the restaurant might be. As he suspected, during the slow time between lunch and dinner, someone from the kitchen was on a break—a young redheaded guy in an apron, smoking outside the back door.

"Pardon me," Alden said, approaching him in a friendly manner.

The previously relaxed kitchen grunt stood up straighter and partially hid his cigarette behind him. "May I help you?"

Good training, Alden thought. "I was just curious about something. Does your kitchen ever prepare picnic lunches that guests can take on carriage rides?"

The young man seemed to relax a bit. "All the time. In fact, we had a big one we were going to do today, but it got canceled."

"What do you consider a big lunch? Just wondering for a ride I'm planning—I want it to be perfect when I pop the question."

The freckled young man grinned. "Better you than me," he said. "We've had people order everything from brie and crackers to steak dinners."

"Is that what you were making today?"

"Naw. Today's was supposed to be lobster with all the trimmings and the world's most expensive cupcake."

"How can a cupcake be expensive?"

"You wouldn't catch me paying seven hundred bucks for a cupcake, but this one has some kind of special Venezuelan chocolate, aged vanilla, one-hundred-year-old cognac and real gold."

"You seem to know a lot about this cupcake," Alden said.

"Wouldn't you be curious? I'd like to be a pastry chef someday, so I looked into it. It came chilled, overnight express from

Las Vegas. Nobody thought to cancel the order, I guess, and now Chef is wondering what to do with it."

"That would have been some carriage ride," Alden remarked.

"Even though all they wanted to drink was organic milk and water." The kid laughed and tucked his cigarette into one of those smoker's posts that acted as an ashtray. "Good luck, man."

"Thanks."

Alden walked back toward the beach, pondering this tidbit. It might be juicy enough for his editor, but he had a feeling he could milk it further. So to speak.

He sat on the sand, got out his new phone and started searching the Internet for "Boyd Bellamy" and "cupcake." Not surprisingly, there were a few prehistoric uses of "cupcake" as a synonym for buxom Hollywood hotties, but on the second page of results, he saw a story about a party Bellamy had hosted in Las Vegas.

He clicked through to the newspaper article. Bellamy had held a birthday party for his then-girlfriend, Mysty Wellington, at one of the tonier Vegas bars. It was quite the bacchanal, apparently, with an elaborate menu that included, for Mysty, one Golden Sin cupcake. It was a special favorite of hers, the story said, and she'd requested it specifically. The description of the treat sounded exactly like the cupcake ordered for the carriage expedition—and besides, how many seven-hundred-dollar cupcakes were there?

Alden's mind reeled. Maybe Bellamy ordered that crazy cupcake for every girlfriend he had.

Or maybe he ordered it especially for Mysty Wellington, who'd been scheduled to be on that carriage ride.

He was scrolling through his contacts for someone who

knew Mysty Wellington's agent when a presence cast a shadow over him. He looked up. It was the skinny manager who'd accosted him before, wielding his tablet like a shield.

"Are you *still* looking for the restaurant?" he asked.

"No, Mr. Frankel," Alden said, getting up. "But I'm about to go there for another meal."

"I didn't see you lurking around the back of the building, did I?"

Wow, he had a sharp eye. Or, more likely, access to security cameras.

"I like to walk a few laps before I eat. Improves the digestion. So if you don't mind?"

"Hmph," Frankel said, but he stepped back and watched Alden walk all the way into the building. Alden knew, because when he looked over his shoulder, Frankel was still there, clutching his tablet, his forehead wrinkled.

He didn't want to eat at Sirenia. It was the middle of the afternoon, and he still wanted to make a few phone calls and try to extract more information out of any guests he ran across. The only way he could do that without looking suspicious was to hang out at the bar. That was where people talked, especially when they started drinking. So he would try to get answers at Lunasea, the resort's indoor-outdoor watering hole. If anyone was hanging out indoors, he'd go there first for the quiet atmosphere that made it easier to talk.

Alden made his way across the lobby and saw that the elegant indoor bar, trimmed out in dark wood, was just busy enough. He copped a barstool, ordered a bourbon and started drinking.

chapter
**fourteen**

ROZ LET herself into her mom's house, still decorated the way she remembered it from her childhood, with beachy bamboo furniture, eccentric lamps and eclectic art. Among the paintings of flowers and beachscapes were black-and-white photos of locations and people around Comet Cove, reflecting her parents' years of newsgathering at the *Courier*.

Roz found her mother dozing on the couch in the living room, covered with a blanket, her silky gray cat Major Tom curled up next to her. The older woman eased herself to a sitting position with difficulty, and Major Tom meowed and jumped down, moving to Roz to rub against her legs.

Her mom's chestnut hair, streaked with gray, was cut short and mussed by the pillow. Where Roz's eyes were hazel, Megan's were a striking gray-green, and they looked tired.

"How you doing today?" Roz asked. "Did I wake you up?"

"It's not a bad day. Just taking a little nap," Megan Melander said. But in her face were now all-too-familiar lines of pain.

Roz went to her and hugged her. "Can I get you something?"

"A ginger ale, if you're getting one for yourself."

"Sure," Roz said, setting down her bag and heading to the kitchen, Major Tom following. She came back a few minutes later with a couple of glasses of soda and a plate of cheese and crackers. And, of course, a salmon treat for Tom, who snatched it from her fingers and disappeared under the couch.

"You know I can't resist cheese," Megan said, helping herself. "Thanks."

"Purely selfish. I can't resist, either." Roz sat on a comfy chair next to the couch and tried not to think about how much worse her mother's progressive MS could get. That someday, even eating might be a problem. But for now, her mom seemed OK, and it was comforting to see her.

"So how's your explosive new story?" Megan asked. She always was one for bad puns.

Roz smiled. "Quite possibly too interesting. And I have some bad news."

"What?" Motherly concern crossed Megan's face.

"I—uh—I lost the boat."

"You lost the boat? You don't even know how to work the boat."

Roz grimaced. "I know. I had help."

"So someone else lost the boat?"

"Not exactly." Roz gave her mother an account of what had happened, leaving out the kiss that she'd been unable to get out of her mind all morning.

"Well, I'm not all that worried about losing the boat since you're OK," Megan said, looking fresher after her snack. Major Tom reemerged, jumped up next to her and studiously licked a paw. "But if we want to collect the insurance, we'll need to report it."

"Probably," Roz replied, "but I'm kind of worried they

aren't going to be all that pleased that we essentially let the boat drive itself across the ocean. I don't want to lie. And I'm not sure if I want to broadcast right now that I was the one out there getting shot at."

"Good point." Megan shrugged. "We can just wait and see if and when it turns up."

"You're not upset?" Roz knew Megan couldn't afford to write off a boat.

Her mother laughed. "Well, I have been wondering how to get rid of it."

"Yeah, but you could use the money."

"I'll be all right." She stroked the cat's back, and he narrowed his golden eyes and purred. "How's circulation?"

"Hits are way up. Too early to tell about circ. But we've had new ad inquiries."

"Good." Megan winced as she shifted on the couch, and Major Tom snuggled closer. "So what do you know? What caused the blast? Give me the scoop."

"There's a theory that the explosion was caused by a spark and a fuel leak. In the short time we had to survey the debris, I didn't get any more ideas. There were no big chunks of boat floating around out there."

"I know what your grandfather would have said."

"Your dad? What?"

"It was a bomb."

Roz shook her head. "Why would anyone bomb the boat?"

"Not that kind of bomb. He always talked about bombs lying all over the floor of the ocean. The gulf, too."

"For real?" Roz pondered the idea. "Is that even possible?"

"I don't know the details, only that he said his own father talked about dumping World War II bombs out there."

"Seems like a real outside chance that a fishing boat could

hook a bomb, but I'll look into it," Roz said. "At least it would make an interesting story on its own, if a bunch of explosives were sitting in the water off Comet Cove."

"Adds a whole new level of excitement to offshore fishing," her mom agreed. "So what's the *Beacon* reporter like?"

"Alden?" Roz scrambled to find something to say. "Arrogant."

"So was your father," Megan said with a knowing smile.

"But in a good way." They both laughed. "I'd better go into the office," Roz said. "We've got to get pages to the printer this afternoon. And maybe I'll look into the bomb angle."

"OK, sweetie. I love you."

"Love you, too, Mom. Thanks."

Later at the office, Roz juggled meetings, freshened the boat story for print and approved pages for transmission to the printer, then devoted herself to editing a story by young Bruce. And cutting five inches out of it, which might just make him cry.

"Roz!"

She snapped her head up to see Janice. "How do you keep sneaking up on me?"

"Because you work like a coal miner, way too hard and in a dark tunnel where all you see is your pickaxe."

Roz snorted. "Chain saw, in this case. What's up?"

"I turned in my story. Do you want to join me for a coffee at Bean Me Up?"

"I don't have time." Roz felt bad. Janice was a friend, but deadline was deadline.

"I thought you'd say that." Janice pulled a paper cup from behind her back and set it on Roz's desk.

"Oh my God. You're a saint." Roz grabbed it and took a sip. Chilled ambrosia. "Mocha!"

"Strings are attached," Janice said. "You're going with me to the jazz fundraiser for the animal shelter at the Moonlight."

"When is that?"

"Next week."

Roz let out a breath. "OK. I think I can do that. Maybe I'll have the stupid boat story nailed by then."

Janice laughed. "You're never done working. But you're going to set aside a Saturday night anyway."

Roz smiled up at her. "You're the best. And I will."

"Good. I'm heading out for my interview at Galileo Gallery." A corner of Janice's mouth turned up. "Have fun playing with Alden Knox."

"What?" Roz exclaimed, but her friend just laughed and walked out the door. Roz had to chuckle. Janice was a *very* good reporter.

Roz sipped her mocha, finished the edit, then finally found a few minutes to do some online research. Information on bombs left under the sea was scattered at best. So instead, she searched for an academic and landed on the website of a retired professor and historian who lived in Bohemia Beach and specialized in twentieth-century Florida history. She shot him an email requesting an interview, then set about approving the last of the *Courier's* pages for Friday publication, wondering what kind of scoop Alden was getting now.

chapter
**fifteen**

ALDEN WAS GETTING the scoop on the wedding of an apparent terrorist named Penny from the men who had just arrived at Lunaria Lodge to stand up for the groom. As he'd sunk deeper into a blissful bourbon haze, which had almost but not quite obliterated his obsessive replaying of this morning's kiss, he'd learned that Penny's bridesmaids had been here all week. The groomsmen, knowing Penny's predilection for enlisting everyone into her wedding army, had put off their "relaxing vacation" until just before the wedding weekend.

Once they got to Comet Cove, however, the men had been unable to escape on their planned fishing trip. The bride had declared that she didn't want half of the wedding party at risk of exploding, no matter how far-fetched the possibility, so she'd forbidden the excursion.

So the groomsmen, five guys in their early twenties who looked as if they'd escaped a high-end catalog, were devastating a bottle of Michter's ten-year-old (and sharing, to Alden's delight). They'd retreated to the bar after Penny asked them to procure live flamingos to stroll around the beach during the ceremony. Apparently her wedding planner had been unable to honor the last-minute request, and the guys weren't planning to raid a zoo to help.

Alden suspected they were about one drink away from doing it anyway.

"You know, there's this store in Bohemia where you can get flamingos," Alden said to his new drinking buddies, who were only too happy to find fresh ears to hear their stories. Unfortunately, none of the tales had to do with Boyd Bellamy.

"You mean you can just buy live flamingos here?" asked the blond best man, who, like the others, was from Connecticut. "That's awesome."

"How about alligators?" his handsome, ebony-skinned friend asked conspiratorially. "That might work."

"They aren't live. The flamingos, I mean," Alden said. "But you can rent a flock of plastic pink flamingos."

The other guys, who'd been engaged in a sidebar about spring training prospects, turned at the words.

"Pink flamingos?"

"A flock of them? How many are in a flock?"

"That would be perfect."

The best man was the only one who looked uncomfortable. "I don't think Penny is going to like it."

"She'll love it," his closest buddy said. "You can't get any more Florida than that."

"I don't know ..."

While they exhorted the best man, Alden poured himself another finger of their three-hundred-dollar whiskey.

"Only if Ray agrees," the best man finally said.

"Ray is never going to agree," said his buddy. "But he is going to *love* it. This can be our gift to him."

More cajoling, more laughter about jokes they'd played on each other in the past, and the best man caved. Before sobriety could make him change his mind, his buddy immediately called the shop (after getting the name from Alden) and reserved two dozen pink flamingos they could pick up tomorrow.

"Penny is going to be pissed," the ambivalent best man lamented.

"You could prime the pump, as it were," Alden then suggested.

The other men snickered.

"What do you mean?" the best man asked.

"Do something in advance to soften her up so she'll dismiss your prank Saturday as boyish enthusiasm rather than malice."

"But what's the fun in that?" another groomsman asked.

"Tell me more," said the best man, gesturing to the bartender for another bottle.

*Excellent,* Alden thought. "I have it on good authority that the restaurant has in its possession a precious cupcake made with rare chocolate, vanilla and gold. It would make a beautiful gift for the bride."

"Really?" the best man said. "A cupcake? That doesn't seem very impressive. Penny is hard to impress."

"It costs about as much as your bar bill, as it currently stands." Alden gestured to the newly opened bottle that had been placed before them.

The blond man's eyebrows shot up. "Then it just might work. I want to see it first, though."

He waved over the bartender, who then waved over the maitre d', who disappeared into the kitchen. Several minutes later, Chef Sofia herself emerged with an elegant bell jar on a silver pedestal. Under the glass dome was a large cupcake, glinting with gold sprinkles, resting in an elaborate blown-sugar bowl. Sculpted sugar bubbles dusted with gold swirled upward in a spiral from its chocolate-frosted top.

"Wow," the drunk guys said as Sofia smiled and set it on the bar.

Alden raised his phone and casually snapped a photo.

"We have to buy this freaking cupcake," the best man said, and the other guys heartily agreed.

"I'll drink to that." Alden finished off his glass, left a tip for the bartender and strolled unsteadily out of the restaurant.

He'd been productive before the groomsmen arrived. He'd used his airline sources to confirm that Mysty Wellington had traveled to Florida last weekend, then used one of his L.A. sources to find the name she used when she checked into hotels. Alden had called every hotel in the area, including this one, asking to speak to her alias. He finally found an upscale boutique hotel in north Comet Cove that said she'd been there but checked out this morning. That was enough to convince Alden that Boyd's date had been none other than his tempestuous ex. Perhaps even more interesting, it appeared she'd been in town the day the boat blew up.

He eased himself out to the beach, sat on the sand and dialed the office. It was just after six, and the sky shifted into shades of rose as the sun sank low, painting the smattering of clouds with coral light. He could get used to these Comet Cove sunsets.

Alden got Kat on the phone and dictated a short story about Boyd's planned but tragically canceled carriage ride and lobster picnic, with ample use of words like "seems" and "suggest" and "sources" to imply that the actor's most likely date was Mysty Wellington, right down to the cupcake. And that Mysty was likely to inherit Boyd's estate, based on his legal tipster.

"I'm emailing you the cupcake photo now," he said. "Get it up with the story as soon as you can."

"Are you sure about this?" Kat asked.

"Absolutely. This is what I do best. At the worst, we've said definitively that Mysty likes really expensive cupcakes. The rest is sourced speculation. It'll be fine."

"For print, OK if I combine this with the story we've got on the boat and Boyd?"

"That would be awesome. Lead with this, though. By tomorrow the boat will be old news." He'd almost forgotten their print product came out tomorrow, Friday, the same day as the *Courier*'s.

"Fine. Send me the photo," Kat said, "and give it ten minutes for the online story to pop up."

"Thanks," Alden replied. "I'll come in and make sure everything looks good for tomorrow."

"John and I will take care of it. Most of the pages are already gone. You should go home."

"You know I like to read the proofs. It makes me feel old-school. *You* should go home. You work too much."

She laughed. "And you drink too much."

"How can you tell?"

"Just don't drive, OK?"

"OK. See ya." He hung up and shot her the photo via email, then stood unsteadily. And saw his favorite manager plodding up the path. "Mr. Frankel, isn't it?" he called. "You have such a beautiful resort here."

Frankel approached him and sniffed suspiciously. "What are you up to?"

"I had a perfect afternoon in your bar," Alden said. "And now I'm going home."

"I'll be happy to call you a cab."

"You sure are helpful," he said, lurching a bit to the left before gaining an upright position.

"I look after our guests," Frankel said with proud authority.

"Tell me something." Alden leaned closer, and Frankel backed away from his bourbon breath. "Do you ever actually *do* anything besides roam the grounds with your tablet of doom?"

Frankel snorted, almost smiling. "And aren't you lucky that I do? Go on up to the front. We'll get you a ride."

"I've got Rideeo. I'm good." But Frankel watched over his shoulder to make sure Alden booked the amateur cabbie before he left him alone.

Fifteen minutes later, with his intoxication fading, Alden rode west and then north in the Toyota Corolla of one of Comet Cove's only rideshare drivers, a pallid young man named Toby. As they rolled over the bridge and through the tropical twilight toward town and his office, he wondered what Roz was up to.

ROZ HAD FINISHED READING and approving the proofs and had started planning next week's edition when her phone buzzed with a text alert from *The Beacon*. She'd signed up for its alerts as soon as she came back to town, but she'd never worried about the gossip rag, as she liked to think of it, scooping her before recently.

Before Alden.

"Crafty rascal," she growled after she clicked over to the website to read his story about the carriage ride and the cupcake. Her sick feeling lessened only slightly as she noted the article contained virtually no confirmed facts but a heck of a lot of circumstantial evidence and unnamed sources.

She'd worked a scant mention of the canceled carriage ride into her print story; it was practically Alden's entire tale. And, she had to admit, it was fascinating.

*This,* she thought, *is why the* Courier *is doomed.*

Perhaps even more annoying than the dubious story was that it left no doubt that Alden was not just clever; he could *write.*

And he could set her on fire, damn him, when he was the last thing she should want.

Mostly, right now, she wanted to smack him.

Roz clutched her head and closed her eyes. She was still exhausted after this morning's ordeal, and now she was hungry. She could tackle the story again tomorrow. She had set up an interview with the historian for 11 a.m.; she'd meet him in Bohemia Beach and take herself out to lunch afterward. For now, she would go home and have a nice dinner of cheese and fruit and wine. Definitely wine.

It was very close to dark, and she'd sent the others home— though they were likely having a few margaritas at Taco Titan, which was kind of a tradition after they put the paper to bed. Normally she'd join them, but tonight, she just didn't have the energy.

As she packed up her bag, Roz contemplated the office, with its years of historic front pages on the walls and desks piled with the comforting clutter peculiar to newspapers. Everywhere was paper, and everywhere were words. Ideas. Stories. And in those stories were people, events, the benchmarks of time, or, as her dad used to quote, "the first draft of history." That was what they were writing. She wanted to do it well.

It would be sad to sell this old place, but it was time. Wasn't it? The world had changed. The world wanted entertainment and gossip and colorful lies and bombastic politicians. There wasn't much room for meticulous storytelling, complexity and the elusive truth.

The thought depressed her a little as she locked up the office and stepped onto the sidewalk outside the *Courier*. The pretty streetlights here didn't cast much of a glow, but she thought she saw movement across the street next to the box office of the darkened theater. She narrowed her eyes and made out a figure standing in the shadows, watching her.

Could it be—Alden? She wanted to frown, but an unbidden smile crept over her face.

And then came squealing tires from out of the alley by her building and a blur of an SUV in front of her. A masked man leapt out of it. Before she could act, he grabbed her arms. She fought back, but she didn't have a chance as two thoughts crossed her mind: She had really messed up. And she was glad she'd met deadline.

And then a thump on her head brought pain and instantaneous darkness.

ALDEN DIDN'T KNOW why he lingered after the Rideeo driver dropped him off near his office.

OK, he did know. The lights were still on at the *Courier,* even though it looked empty, and that meant someone was still working. And who else would be the last one to leave but a dedicated, old-school newspaperman in a woman's body?

A body he suddenly, in his still-tipsy state, wanted to see again.

He leaned against the wall inside one of the dark alcoves on either side of the Moonlight Theater's closed box office and played with his phone for a few minutes, checking his story. Then he sensed a change in the light. He pocketed his phone and looked up. The *Courier's* lights had been turned out, and Roz was locking the door. And to his surprise and delight, she swiveled and peered across the street in his direction.

He took a tiny step forward so the streetlight caught him.

She smiled.

And then a black SUV roared out of the alley next to the newspaper's squat building and screeched to a halt between them.

He couldn't see her, but he knew she was in trouble. A faint cry confirmed it. The blast of adrenaline sobered him instantly.

"Roz!" Alden sprinted across the street, running toward the vehicle, hoping she was OK on the other side.

In those few seconds, he heard the sounds of a struggle and a man's voice yelling, "Hurry!"

Alden hurtled around the back of the car and came across a man entirely in black, mask and all, trying to drag Roz into the SUV's open back door.

"Get away from her!" Alden yelled, leaping forward and punching the masked man in the chin.

Surprised, the guy staggered back, dropping Roz, mumbling curses in a peculiar gravelly voice, as another shadowed man inside the car said: "Forget it! Come on!"

Roz lay on the sidewalk, not moving. Panting, furious, Alden stood between her and her attacker, who apparently thought better of whatever he was trying to do and jumped into the SUV, slamming the door as it squealed away. The tinted windows revealed nothing more, and Alden caught only the first few letters of the license plate.

He cursed, dropped to his knees and put a finger to Roz's neck. She had a pulse. She was breathing. "Roz." He squeezed her shoulders, lifting her to cradle her head in his lap. "Roz, can you hear me? Oh, God, Roz, wake up. Wake up!" He fumbled in his pocket for his phone, getting ready to call 9-1-1, when she shifted against him and groaned.

"What happened?" Her eyes drifted open, at first sleepy and confused, then wide and terrified. "Alden?"

"Someone attacked you. Do you know what they did to you? Did they stick a needle into you or anything?"

She palmed her temple. "I think they hit me in the head. Are they gone?"

"They're gone. I interrupted them. I guess they didn't want to deal with you *and* a drunk, pissed-off reporter."

Roz coughed out a chuckle. "Yeah. You might interview them to death."

He cracked a smile despite his worry and looked around. The street was quiet, for now. "I need to get you out of here, in case they come back. But I should probably call an ambulance."

"Don't," Roz croaked, sitting up. "Ouch." She touched her head again.

"You could have a concussion or worse."

"I'm fine. I think it was the shock of it more than anything. I just want to go home."

"I'm not leaving you alone," Alden said. "I'll take you home with me. If you're the target, they won't go after you at my place."

"Target for what? This makes no sense."

"Yeah, it's made no sense twice today."

"You smell like booze," Roz said, wrinkling her nose. "You can't drive."

"Don't worry. I've got a guy," Alden said, tapping his phone, summoning the driver who'd just dropped him off. This time he texted Toby's personal number, which he already had in his phone. He liked having contacts all over town; he never knew when he might need them. And he needed Toby now. This way there wouldn't be a record in the rideshare company's files, just in case the people after Roz were wily enough to ask. And he'd give the kid a good tip.

Roz closed her eyes again, then let Alden lift her to her

feet. He clutched her arms, holding her steady, noting her weary look, her disheveled hair. "You sure you're OK?"

"Just completely freaked out. Where's my bag?"

Alden looked around. "Is this it?" he asked, picking up the leather satchel that rested askew against the wall.

"Yes, thanks." She took it from him and held it tight, as if it were a security blanket.

"Here's Toby," Alden said as the Corolla pulled up. Alden helped her into the back seat, slid in next to her and gave Toby the address.

Alden wrapped an arm around Roz, and she rested her head against his shoulder. Her easy acquiescence worried him more than anything. It was as if all the fight had gone out of her. And he liked her full of fight. "We can go right up the road to the ER if you want," he said softly.

"No, Mr. Knox, I'm fine," she said.

He smiled, holding her a little more closely. "What about the police?"

She looked up at Alden and then glanced at the driver, and he got the message. *Not now.*

In a moment, she was dozing against him. He didn't dare move as he listened to her soft breathing and the car rumbled south.

When they got to his place, Alden eased his arm off Roz, pulled a wad of cash from his wallet, and reached between the seats to hand it to Toby. "Thanks."

"Thank *you*! This is twice what I'd get from Rideeo. Call anytime. Just don't tell on me." Toby grinned, his eyes lighting up underneath his font of curly dark bangs.

"Right back at you. Let's keep this just between us, OK?"

"I got you. She OK?" Toby eyed Roz, who still seemed groggy.

"She bumped her head."

Roz sat straight up, and her eyes snapped open. "I'm fine!"

Alden chuckled. "Apparently she's fine. I'll take good care of her."

"All right," Toby said. "Have a good night."

Roz was already opening her door, but Alden jumped out his side and ran around the car to help her out.

"So noble," she said dryly. She looped the strap of her bag over her head as Toby buzzed away.

"Someone's feeling better," he quipped. But Roz didn't object when he guided her up the stairs and inside his place.

It was an airy little apartment, with lots of windows and a kitchen that opened into the living space. "Little" was the operative word, and he'd furnished it simply, with comfortable modern pieces, stuffed bookcases, a TV and very little bric-a-brac.

Alden guided Roz to the couch. She shrugged off his arm and sank into the cushions with a sigh, closing her eyes again.

"Last call for a doctor," he said.

"Not unless someone attacks us again."

"Hope they wait till tomorrow. Can I get you something?"

"Any kind of soda with real sugar would be good," she said. "I need fizz."

"Root beer, coming right up."

Alden retrieved two IBCs out of the fridge, handed her one bottle and took a sip from the other as he sat next to her. She took a long swallow, and he told himself he shouldn't be distracted by her red lips as she drank. But he was anyway.

Roz sighed as she lowered the bottle. He let out a long breath, tearing his eyes away from her mouth. *Get a grip, Alden.*

"Should I call the police?" he asked her after a moment.

"Not now. But I'll file a report in the morning. About the boat, too."

"Maybe that's how they found you," Alden said.

She looked at him, and he noted her color seemed much better, her voice steadier. "What do you mean?"

"If the guys who shot at us this morning got the registration number off your boat, there would be ways to track down the registrant."

"But my name wouldn't be on the record. Oh, God, would they go after my mom?"

"They didn't," Alden reassured her. "They made the connection with you for a reason. If they knew it was your family's boat, it would be easy enough to find out about your connection to the *Courier*. You're the editor. You were the target. The first time, they might not have known who you were—"

"But this time, the bastards knew exactly who I was." She shook her head. "But why? Again, why? What am I doing that's ticking somebody off? And they almost—they almost kidnapped me."

She shuddered, and Alden shifted closer to her, sliding an arm around her shoulders.

"It's unnerving," he said, "but we'll tell the police, and we'll figure it out. It may be they just wanted to scare you off something you're writing."

"There are other ways to scare somebody, Alden." Her eyes were wide, gold flecked with green, as her gaze caught his. "They—I think they wanted to kill me."

"Shhh," he said, holding her closer, and she rested her head on his shoulder again. Even as his body responded to her warmth, fury boiled up within him at the thought that anyone would try to harm her.

For what? What was in her stories that had someone scared or angry enough to kill? After all, he was more likely to annoy people with his gossip pieces. Her bylines this week included the boat explosion, sure, but she'd also written about city council votes, a legal dispute between neighbors, even a lost dog reunited with its family. He'd envied her light touch with that really cute story. But he couldn't imagine any of those articles prompting these attacks.

Or maybe it was just Roz's and his presence this morning in the ocean, when they didn't even know what they were looking for. The shooters, whoever they were, had seen them and deemed them a threat. Once they figured out Roz was connected with the newspaper, they must have decided she had to be eliminated. Maybe it *was* drug dealers.

"You're squeezing me pretty hard, Alden," Roz said in an amused voice.

"Sorry." He eased his grip and patted her shoulder. "Just thinking about why someone would do this to you. There must have been something at the accident scene we weren't supposed to see."

"Oh, crap! That reminds me."

"What?"

Roz wriggled as she reached into her pocket. Her movement against his thigh shot an arcing lightning bolt right to his groin.

"I have this." She held up a tiny memory card. "From the camera. I haven't tried to read it yet. It got wet, but these things have a reputation for surviving a lot."

"Do you mind if we look at it?"

"Do I mind? Oh, because you're the competition?" She paused, as if she were coming to a decision. "At this point,

Alden, I'm happy to share, as long as I don't put you in danger."

"Nice of you," he said. "Relax. I'll get my laptop."

He retrieved the computer and a card reader, which he plugged into a USB port. Roz slipped the SD card into the slot, and after a few seconds of suspense, the photo program pulled up rows of thumbnails.

Roz exhaled.

"Excellent," Alden said.

The small images didn't show much, but Alden hit the import button and let it work so they would be able to see the larger pictures.

Roz made a strange sound, and Alden turned to see her clutching her belly.

"Did they punch you in the stomach, too? Are you OK?"

She gave him an embarrassed smile. "I'm just hungry."

"Me, too. Bourbon, it turns out, does not provide adequate nutrition, even excellent bourbon."

"Should I ask?" Roz said.

"It was all for journalism." Alden picked up his phone and looked up Pluto's Pizza. "Dinner coming right up."

AS THEY WAITED for the pizza, they looked at the imported photos. There weren't that many, and Roz's flash had mostly glinted off unidentifiable pieces of debris. A few were obviously boat parts. There appeared to be pieces of cushion, plastic and netting, along with irregular shapes that, even with the flash, were a mystery.

"And a lot of it probably sank," said Roz, whose head was feeling much better after the infusion of root beer and the promise of dinner.

"I thought the same thing," Alden said. "No smoking gun, then."

"I don't know. Something seems off, but I can't put my finger on it." She frowned as she scrolled to the last frame. "And this boat photo sucks."

"Hang on." Alden adjusted a few settings, and they could see the shape of the boat that had pursued them more clearly. Still, it gave them no clue who it was.

There was a knock, and Roz looked at the door nervously. Alden got up and peeked out the window first, opened the door and exchanged cash for a box of what appeared to be steaming, cheesy deliciousness as he opened it on his coffee table. The accompanying scent of garlic was heavenly.

"Mmmm. I want to marry this pizza right now," Roz said after savoring the first bite. It was as scrumptious as it smelled.

"I just want to watch you eat it and make that noise again," Alden teased, and she smacked his arm. He laughed. "No need to get violent."

"Maybe if I'd been a little more violent, I wouldn't have been bashed in the head."

"Did you see them coming? Did you recognize either of them?"

"No. Actually, I was looking at you."

"Oh." Alden sounded sheepish. "Sorry. I guess I looked kind of like a stalker, didn't I? But I assure you, I was just drunk. I didn't recognize them either, but it didn't help that the guy with the froggy voice wore a mask. Froggy's friend was in the shadows."

"Froggy—I vaguely remember hearing that voice now. It sounded like his throat was full of rocks. But I don't recall what they said or what they looked like. I'm glad you were watching me, or I might be—" Roz paused, unwilling to contemplate what might have happened. She started shaking and put down the crust of the slice she'd just about polished off.

Alden took one look at her, set down his slice and wrapped both arms around her, pulling her close. He caressed her hair, and she was instantly distracted. And embarrassed.

"Shhh," he said in her ear. "You're all right. And I'm not going to let anything happen to you."

Her shaking eased after a minute under the influence of his body's heat and the soothing sound of his voice. He felt so good.

And this was so dangerous.

Roz might be willing to work with Alden, but she didn't need to *hook up* with him. A one-night stand would be awkward, and more—more would make it harder to leave Comet Cove, which she wanted to do before the year was out. And the very thought of "more" was ridiculous. He was the enemy, wasn't he?

With effort, she pulled away from him.

"Alden, I don't expect you to rescue me ever again. I'll be all right. Maybe these guys will back off when we file a police report on this. Or the sheriff will call in extra help from the county. At the very least, no one wants the VIPs in town to be any more alarmed than they already are."

Alden shrugged. "I can't let something bad happen to you. I'm invested in you now. You're my partner. Maybe my conscience." He sported a mischievous smile, but there was something behind it, something a little sad.

"Don't you have your own conscience?"

"It's taken a beating," he said simply, picking up his pizza.

As they ate, they flipped through websites that had news about Boyd Bellamy and talked over the angles. Nobody had as much as they had—or as much as Alden had, she thought. Some of the gossip sites were already quoting his latest story.

"Even the fishing company seems convinced the explosion was caused by a fuel leak," Roz said. "I mean, they said they were still looking into it, but that was the subtext I got."

"You'd think they'd be avoiding any kind of conclusion at this point," Alden replied. "Blaming God or lightning or a meteor from space, anything so that their customers wouldn't see their boats as unsafe."

"Or maybe they just want this to go away as quickly as possible."

"What could be more damaging to their rep than shoddy safety?" Alden asked.

"I don't know. Wouldn't it be interesting if it were a different kind of accident? My mom suggested I look into another possibility. It's a real outside chance, but I thought it might make a story in and of itself. If you want, you can come with me tomorrow morning for the interview."

"What possibility?"

"Unexploded munitions dumped into the ocean."

Alden lifted an eyebrow. "Is that a thing? And if so, how would it affect these guys? Did they have a submarine skimming the bottom?"

"Maybe we'll find out tomorrow, if you're up for it."

"Wouldn't miss it."

"Good." The idea of having company after tonight's scare was reassuring. She yawned. What a day. "I'm pretty tired. Thanks for the pizza—and the rescue. I should go home."

"Hell, no." Alden's look was fierce. "If they know where you work, they know where you live. You can't go home yet, at least not until we get the cops involved."

"But Alden—"

"No 'buts.'" He looked her over, and she saw something in his eyes, an earnestness. Protectiveness, even. This was ridiculous. This wasn't a big, strong man who existed for her protection. This was Alden Knox, obnoxious rival reporter.

Who happened to be rather big and strong.

"You'll sleep in my bed. I'll sleep on the couch," he said in answer to her raised eyebrows.

Roz shook her head. "Just like in the movies? No need to be that gallant. I insist on the couch. I've put you out enough already."

"But—"

"No 'buts,' right?" She smiled. "Have a blanket and a pillow?"

Emotions warred on his face before he relented. "I'll get them."

While Alden went to retrieve bedding, Roz went to the bathroom. Business accomplished, she examined her head in the mirror. There was a subtle bump and a slight ache, but it wasn't too bad. She blamed fright as much as the attack for her fainting. She had the same reaction if she looked at the vial when she had blood drawn.

She found some mouthwash and rinsed, then returned to the living room. Alden had spread sheets on the couch, along with a pillow and a quilt.

"You know, you can still sleep in my bed," Alden said, flirting again. "You wouldn't even have to kick me out first."

"Ha ha," said Roz, but his words gave her a rush as her imagination went wild. She shook off the image. "Wake me in the morning. We'll have to get back to my car so we can drive to the interview. Where's yours, anyway?"

"Up at Lunaria Lodge."

"I'll take you to it later, if that's OK."

"Good idea," Alden said. "My boss won't appreciate it if you're driving me to all my interviews."

Roz smiled. "This is a temporary truce." She sat on the couch, pulled off her shoes and socks and looked up at him, at his handsome face, as tired as hers. She felt vulnerable. And grateful. "Thank you."

"See you in the morning," he said softly and went to his bedroom.

She closed his laptop and turned off the light. Then she wriggled out of her jeans and removed her bra, more comfortable in just her shirt and underpants as she snuggled between the sheets and quilt, all too aware of the man in the next room.

And the darkness. And the wind picking up, rushing through the trees, knocking branches against the windows. Hints of yellow streetlights seeped through the blinds, and the world outside seemed very close and very scary as she slipped into restless sleep.

THE STRANGE CRY woke Alden from a troubled slumber. It took a moment for him to get oriented. In his dream, he'd been on Roz's boat, trying to drive them away from a man o' war, an English frigate with billowing sails. It was firing cannons at them, all smoke and noise and hurtling projectiles.

The sound stopped, and he sat up and remembered where he was and who was in his apartment.

There was a shadow in the doorway of his bedroom.

"Roz?"

"Alden?"

"Are you OK?"

"Nightmares," she said. "I thought someone was breaking in."

He slipped out of bed by the light of the clock—2:24 a.m.—and padded over to her in his boxers, wincing at each touch of his bare, battered feet on the wooden floor. The cool air raised goose bumps on his naked torso.

She was in his room.

She was nervous, yes. But she was in his room.

He tried not to assume what he couldn't help but think. Want.

"Hang on a sec," he said. "I'm going to take a look."

"Be careful," she said. "But I think it was just a dream."

This whole experience felt like a dream as he peeked through the closed blinds on every window and made sure no one was at his door. It didn't seem like anyone was out there.

He went back to the bedroom, where Roz stood with her arms crossed, looking cold.

"Come here," he whispered, and he wrapped his arms around her. "Must have been some dream."

She rested her head against his chest with a shiver. "I'm not used to being scared."

"It's easier to pretend not to be."

"I'll have to try it," she said, the strain in her voice easing. He felt her warm breath against him and rubbed his hands across her back. Her skin was smooth through the soft cotton of her shirt. He became aware of her nude legs against his and realized she was in her underwear, with nothing under her shirt, and his body responded. He shifted, not wanting her to know how much he wanted her.

"You're safe," he said. "It's OK."

"Is it?" Roz faced him, looked up at him, and in the dim light, he saw her eyes were wide and moist and skeptical. But they held something else. Yearning. The same light he'd seen the other night after dinner, when she'd practically run away. "Maybe—" She stepped backward. "I'm going back to the couch. I just wanted to see if you heard the noise."

"I heard only you." And the wind. It rushed through the trees outside in a wave of sound that made the night feel exquisitely alive.

He reached out, gently lifted her chin, and she froze and looked up at him. But she didn't run this time. He leaned in slowly and, with barely a second's pause, took her mouth with his. Roz sighed into his kiss, and he felt the thrill of her surrender to the moment. To him. She curved into his embrace like a willow in a breeze, and she slipped her arms around his waist. God, she tasted good, and that whiff of jasmine she carried with her wrapped him up in a gossamer cloud of heat and hormones and want. She opened her mouth to him, and he slipped his tongue inside, finding hers, tilting his head to capture her more fully.

And then she pulled away with a gasp. "Bad idea."

"But such a *good* bad idea," he said, aching at losing her delicious heat. "Stay with me."

"We can't do this. Not—we just can't."

She was going to say "not now." Did that mean they *could* do this? Maybe it was just a matter of convincing her, even if it wasn't tonight. He had no idea why he wanted her so much, his snooty rival. Only she was becoming a lot more than that, and he didn't like that thought, either. Maybe slowing things down was the way to go.

He held up his hands. "Look, that couch isn't that comfortable. I should know. I've passed out on it before."

Her mouth quirked up. "You're not really selling yourself here."

Alden chuckled. "Come to the bed. I'll behave myself. And … you'll be safe."

She raised an eyebrow, as if to mock his declaration. But she also didn't say no. "I suppose I can behave myself, too."

He barked out a laugh at her unexpected response and gestured toward the bed. "This way, my lady."

"So chivalrous." She moved to the least rumpled side of the bed and slipped under the covers, eyeing him. Unreadable. Beautiful in the blue glow of the clock and the scant yellow light filtering around the blinds.

He hoped she didn't get a good look at his boxers as he moved to the other side, grabbed a fleece throw from the soft chair in the corner and pulled it over himself, on top of the covers. He was too hot and bothered to consider getting under them with her. Not yet. They had a deal.

"This feels like a romance novel," she said, turning to face him as they both nestled into the pillows. "I didn't think people did this in real life. Sleeping in the same bed with a blanket separating us."

"We can rewrite the book any time. Just say the word."

"I do like the steamier novels best."

He bit back a groan as she looked into his eyes and grinned.

Alden stretched an arm over her—over the blankets—and pulled her closer. "Is this all right?"

"Yes." It came out as a breathy whisper.

He moved even closer. Closer still. Touched her lips lightly with his. Then retreated to his pillow, treasuring this fragile moment as she closed her eyes and sighed. This would have to be enough, for now. It was certainly more than he expected.

He didn't think she was scared anymore as calm overtook them. Her hair sprawled over the pillow as she nestled against him and almost instantly fell into the even breaths of sleep. But with his arms full of her curves, even through the blanket, Alden realized how much turmoil had been unleashed in his heart.

And it rocked him to his core.

ROZ'S EYES opened at the smell of coffee. Good coffee.

They opened wider when she remembered where she was and in what condition: in Alden Knox's bed. She still had clothes on. That was something.

Then again, those kisses had been something, too. And Alden, so protective. So freaking hot. And the way he'd held her, close and tender, made her feel as if nothing bad could touch her.

But now the morning sun spilled around the closed blinds, and she could hear him in the kitchen, and they were going to have to work together while working for competing newspapers. She'd agreed to that, too, in a moment of weakness.

Then again, she'd almost been killed last night, and he'd saved her, and that moment was a powerful thing.

Now all the fear and confusion came back to her, too, all the questions surrounding this nutty story—if the attempts on her life even had to do with the story, which she was starting to doubt.

Her bra and jeans were in the living room. She needed to get home and change before she did anything.

She snuck into the bathroom, then tried to make a quiet foray into the living room. But with no walls between it and the kitchen, it was kind of hard to be stealthy.

"Good morning, Ms. Melander," came the voice she was starting to know so well.

She turned to face him, determined not to be embarrassed as she stood there in her underwear. "So we're back to that, are we?"

Alden was dressed, put together in khakis and a white shirt, his debonair hair still wet from a shower. His look of cool amusement morphed into something else as he took her in. He set down his coffee cup, and his gray eyes flashed silver. "May I do something for you?" His voice was throaty.

Her face burned, and a low fire kindled in her core. "I'm fine," she whispered, then whirled to grab her jeans and put them on.

"You don't have to rush," he drawled. He moved back to the kitchen. "Coffee?"

"Yes, please. And I think we do have to rush." With pants on, she struggled to don her bra while not fully removing her shirt. Then she realized how ridiculous she looked when she caught the smile tugging at the corner of his mouth. He turned toward the coffee maker, and she scooted into the bedroom to get dressed like a normal person.

She returned to the couch to don her socks and shoes. Ugh. Day-old underwear and socks. She really wanted to go home and reset her morning.

"It's ready," Alden called. Roz walked over to the kitchen, and he handed her a heavy white ceramic mug that said "Write On." She took a tentative sip and looked at him in wonder.

Mocha.

"Do you need ice?" he asked.

"No—this is good." Wow. He'd actually noticed what she ordered for coffee in the morning, when she thought he'd been flirting with Lily. Well, he probably had been flirting with Lily, but still. The drink warmed her in more ways than one.

"Breakfast?" he asked.

"No time." The microwave clock said 8:15 a.m. "We need to get my car from downtown, and then I want to shower and change, and then we have to file a report at the station and get to my interview in Bohemia Beach, the one I told you about. If you still want to come," she added, giving him an out.

"Of course."

"OK, great," she said, trying to sound convincing.

Alden stared her down, taking another sip of coffee. "Shall I summon our driver?"

Ten minutes later, Toby was back in Alden's driveway, and they were on their way north over the bridge to downtown through the cool morning, paging through the two papers that had been delivered to Alden's doorstep: the *Courier* and *The Beacon*. Seated side by side, they shot each other glances as they read the stories, pretending they weren't spying on each other. Finally, Roz got to the classifieds of her own paper and took a moment to glance over the personals.

"Looking for someone?" Alden teased.

"Old habit," Roz said. "It's kind of calming to see everyone desperately searching."

"We're all alone together," Alden agreed as they rolled into town and pulled up outside the *Courier*.

Funny, Roz thought. She'd never thought of Alden as philosophical.

It was windy and cloudier than yesterday as a cold front pushed past Comet Cove. Still, it was a pleasant day; cold fronts rarely had much of a bite here. Roz hopped out of the amateur cab, took a breath of the fresh air and quickly entered her car.

Alden, however, took his time, making her plan to avoid the walk of almost-shame almost impossible. He called out a boisterous "Good morning!" to her painfully prompt co-worker Bruce, who shot her a strange look as he walked up to the *Courier* building. The business staff, of course, was already in there, probably staring out the window and wondering what was going on.

"Are you trying to make things difficult?" Roz asked when Alden finally got into the car.

"I have no idea what you mean."

She couldn't exactly accuse him of trying to get her fired. She *was* the boss. But her co-workers didn't need to know everything about her personal life. Alden, as usual, was pulling her virtual pigtails.

She drove south and back over the causeway to her rented bungalow, and they looked around for suspicious characters before exiting the car and going into the house. Roz invited Alden to sit in the living room while she took a shower and changed—conscious the entire time of his presence in the next room. Irreproachably polite, he didn't even tease her about joining her.

*What's so wrong with me?* she wondered. Then she had to laugh at herself. This was what she'd wanted—his distance. Or at least, that was what she'd told him.

This was why she hadn't wanted to sleep with him: the second-guessing. The professional muddle. Even so, scared and lonely in the middle of the night, facing mortality and tempted by his valiant, intoxicating presence, she'd gone to him. Sure, they'd maintained a barrier between them, literally, but she hadn't ever let herself get so close to intimacy with someone she barely knew. It could have gone either way. There was no denying she'd been watching Alden for a month like a ravenous dog eyeing a steak.

She wasn't a one-night-stand kinda girl, but she had to admit the couple of boyfriends in her past had been, well, boring. Convenient for dates and holidays. Convenient for companionship.

Alden wasn't boring, but he certainly wasn't convenient. And even if he weren't a rake, he was the competition. She had to remember that.

Roz emerged from her bedroom in opaque charcoal leggings and a matching long, scoop-neck dress that fit her bodice and flared around her legs, with a slit that ran all the way up her thigh. Black boots and a long silver necklace and earrings completed the power outfit, which was concealing and provocative at the same time.

"Wow," Alden said appreciatively as she picked up her bag. He put down the magazine he was reading and stood, almost twitching, as if he wanted to touch her and was holding himself back.

She smiled and hefted the bag she'd packed in case she had to escape to a hotel. "Ready to go?"

He nodded.

Next: another trip over the bridge to the sheriff's office downtown, which smelled of burnt coffee and bustled with officers coming and going. Duke was out, to Roz's chagrin, but Deputy Byrd agreed to take their report. With varying degrees of disbelief, scolding for not reporting the shooting earlier, and sympathy and alarm at the kidnapping attempt, Deputy Byrd took down the details, including the first few letters of the license plate that Alden got.

"When were you going to tell us about the boat?" Deputy Byrd asked Roz again, her voice severe.

"I was worried reporting it might make me a target," Roz said.

"And we can see how that worked out."

"Take it easy," Alden interrupted. "We're telling you what we know so you can keep an eye out for whoever is targeting Roz."

"And why would anyone target you?" the deputy said, slightly less stern.

"That's what we'd like to find out," Roz said.

"I suggest you take precautions," the deputy said. "Don't go anywhere alone. Don't put yourself in a vulnerable position. You might even engage a bodyguard. There's a security firm in Bohemia I can recommend. And *don't* visit crime scenes without talking to us first." Roz nodded as she continued. "We'll step up patrols and see what we can get out of the license plate, but this doesn't give us a lot to go on. Does your office have security cameras?"

"No," Roz said, thinking that was one more amenity she couldn't afford.

"Consider getting them. And you"—Deputy Byrd turned to Alden—"don't be a hero. Call the police."

"If you're referring to last night, there wasn't time," he said.

"You could have called us right afterward."

Roz spoke. "We had to sort some things out. Is that all, deputy? We have another appointment."

"You do, do you?" She looked from one of them to the other, obviously realizing it was kind of unusual for reporters from two different papers to have an appointment together. "Anything we should know about?"

"*Courier* business," Roz said.

"You may go," Deputy Byrd said, entertained by Roz's impatience. "But I have some information that might be of interest first."

Roz and Alden waited while the officer tapped through windows on her computer, then went over to another table to pull a piece of paper off the printer.

She handed it to Roz. "Look familiar?"

It was a report of a flaming husk of a boat grounded on the

shores of Seabranch Preserve. The description matched Roz's missing Grady-White.

"Where's Seabranch Preserve?" Alden asked, reading over her shoulder.

"It's a beachfront state park in Stuart," Roz said. "Lots of wildlife. So, uh, it didn't hurt anyone?"

"Only your pocketbook, apparently," Deputy Byrd said with her first real smile.

At least someone was amused, Roz thought. "So the boat is toast, and my camera really is lost. I thought, maybe, if I was lucky—"

"I think it's safe to say that this week, 'lucky' is not among your attributes," Alden said.

"So I won't buy any lottery tickets." Roz tried to control her irritation. She turned to the deputy. "How did my boat get to be in that condition? Was it anything like the Boyd Bellamy accident?"

"You mean, did it blow up?" the officer said. "Nothing so exciting. It appears it was deliberately torched, though the boaters who found it noted a few bullet holes."

"Fabulous." Roz grimaced. "Thank you, Deputy Byrd. We'll be in touch."

"As will we," the officer said, still smiling as the pair left.

"Was she serious about hiring a bodyguard?" Roz asked when they got outside. "That would drive me crazy. How would I be able to report anything? And is it just me, or does she seem to take a perverse pleasure in other people's pain?"

"Maybe she just hates journalists," Alden said. "You really can't blame her."

Roz chuckled as they walked toward her car. "You can't blame people for hating *you*," she said. "I, on the other hand, am a responsible reporter and all-around nice girl."

"Are you really?" Alden smirked.

Heat shot through her, and her gaze snapped to his. A small smile played about his lips, making light of his teasing. But she saw the fire in his eyes.

She swallowed and unlocked the car. "Let's head north, to Bohemia Beach."

QUENTIN RODEBAUGH LIVED in an apartment above a detached, two-car garage. It squatted next to a beautifully restored Mediterranean Revival home in the older, richer part of Bohemia Beach. A grand old live oak tree spread its wizened arms over the yard, and stately royal palms lined the drive.

A couple of service vehicles sat in the wide driveway. Roz parked on the street so she wouldn't block anyone in—and to keep a low profile.

"I wonder if the *Bugle* is sniffing around this story," Roz said as they exited her car and walked up the drive. The *Bohemia Bugle* had some overlap with her coverage area, but it was more concerned with stories north of Comet Cove's city limit, all the way up to the space center.

"They ran a short piece on the explosion, but I haven't seen any follow-ups," Alden said.

"Good." She and Alden exchanged a grin.

They ascended the staircase outside the garage and knocked. They were answered by the yapping of a dog and a gruff, "Be quiet, Auggie." After a moment, the door opened, revealing a stocky, sixtysomething man with thin, flyaway white hair, a bristling gray beard and a not-so-gently-loved gray cardigan over a black St. Augustine T-shirt. Jeans and tattered canvas sneakers completed the retired academic outfit.

Quentin's rough red face had seen too much of the Florida sun, Roz thought, but his blue eyes were bright, and they lit up with his smile as he welcomed them in. At his feet, a dachshund yipped. The shy dog let Roz pet him, sniffed Alden with suspicion and then cowered behind his master.

"Very interesting subject you're writing about, Ms. Melander," said Quentin, leading them into his cluttered, bookcase-lined sitting room after the introductions. She saw Alden suppress a smile at his formal use of her name.

"Call me Roz," she said, shooting Alden a quelling look. "I was hoping you might be able to help us."

"Of course. Sit down, won't you?"

Quentin sat in a comfy chintz chair that had a pink crocheted piece sewn into the back where his head would rest. Created by whom, she wondered. His late wife? Roz had done a little digging and knew he was a widower with no children.

Next to the chair, like most of the surfaces in the room, an end table overflowed with books. Roz had to move a pile of books from the threadbare, flowery couch so she and Alden could both sit down, but one end of the sofa was still so crowded with pillows and magazines that he had to sit close to her. Or maybe he simply chose to sit that close, and she was torn between annoyance and a buzz of happiness.

She tried to ignore the feel of his warm thigh against hers and focus on the task at hand. She pulled a notebook from her bag. Alden didn't take out his phone. He was letting her lead on this one.

"I saw you've done some research into local military history," Roz said. "I wanted to ask about unexploded bombs and whether there might be any in the ocean."

Quentin laughed, and his little dog jumped onto his lap. "Oh, yes. Oh, my, yes. Both the Atlantic and the gulf were dumping grounds after World War II, and not just American bombs. All kinds of UXOs—unexploded ordnance."

"How much are we talking about?" Alden asked.

"Well, that's the thing. No one really knows. The military doesn't even know. But some pretty smart fellows have guessed there's, say, thirty million pounds of it out there in the gulf on the west side of the state, and more in the Atlantic, including very sensitive dumps of chemical weapons."

"All that is just off *Florida?*" Roz asked in disbelief as Alden grunted.

"Oh, yes. There's more off our other coastlines, but we have quite a bit of it here."

She didn't like the sound of that. "But where is it? Is any of it nearby?"

"Well, again, it's hard to say just where it is," Quentin said, stroking the back of his little dog, who closed his eyes and basked in the attention. "We know there are concentrations off the Texas and Louisiana coasts, but not all of it has been mapped. Much of it is, say, fifty miles out or more. More has been mapped off Cape Canaveral and south."

"South? Like here? There wouldn't be some about ten miles off Comet Cove, would there?" Roz asked.

"I don't see why there wouldn't be," the professor said in his jovial manner. "That's the southern end of one documented dumping ground. And the stuff does move around. Authorities had to blow up a bomb found on the beach near Tampa last year. Besides, a lot of it was dumped in uncharted places, and if a pilot was feeling lazy one day, they might have decided to drop it just offshore."

"But why would they do that?" Roz asked. "Didn't they know it was dangerous?"

"They simply didn't imagine anyone would be interacting with the sea floor. But now with more oil drilling proposed out there, there's concern that speculators blasting the sea floor with scouting equipment—seismic airguns, I believe they're called—will blow the munitions apart and compromise old nerve-gas canisters and the like."

"Holy cannoli," Alden said. "But they haven't dumped munitions since World War II?"

"I'm afraid that's incorrect," Quentin said. "The surpluses started after the war. Dumping didn't stop until 1970."

"What?" Roz and Alden asked together.

Perversely, Quentin laughed again. "I don't know why you're surprised. The sea is still, sadly, the world's trash bin." Auggie the dog rolled onto his back on Quentin's lap and basked in a belly rub. "The practice is banned now, but it's too late. The chemical weapons may be the worst. No doubt they're leaking after years under the water. And then there are the land mines and the classic bombs."

"Classic bombs?" Alden asked archly.

"Well, you know, the large UXOs, two hundred fifty to a thousand pounds. Some of them are the size of refrigerators. You don't want to catch that in your fishing net or run into them when you're installing a new drilling platform." Quentin chuckled as Roz wrote furiously.

There was silence for a moment as she caught up. "You mentioned fishing nets. So a charter fishing boat might trigger one of these bombs?"

"Well, I'm not much of a fisherman, but they don't use the big nets, do they?" Quentin said.

Alden shook his head. "Bait nets, if anything, and they barely dip below the surface."

"What about an anchor?" Roz asked. "Could that set off a bomb?"

"Perhaps if you were especially unlucky," the professor said.

"They'd have to have a long anchor chain or be in water that wasn't that deep," Alden speculated.

"*And* be in just the right spot," Quentin replied. "Though there are shoals offshore—shallower areas. Now if you were really cursed, your anchor or a fishing line might tangle with a large fishing net and pull one of those bombs to the surface, and then—well—"

"Boom," Alden said. He and Roz exchanged a glance.

Could the Consummate Catch boat have been that unlucky? "Sounds like a shot in a million," Roz said.

Quentin nodded. "Quite."

They got a little more background from the professor, along with his bona fides and an exhaustive summary of the book he was writing about the home front in Florida during World War II, before leaving him and the snoozing Auggie.

"He seemed pretty amused by the idea of blowing stuff up," Alden remarked after they got into her car.

"I suppose life is a comedy or a tragedy," Roz said, heading for a famous local burrito shop where they could grab lunch. "He chooses to view it as a comedy."

"Until his fishing boat runs into a World War II bomb the size of a refrigerator."

"I think even a smaller bomb would do it, but do you think that's what happened?"

"The anchor-fishing-net scenario?" Alden mused. "It's not

that much weirder than a fuel leak, now that we know there are millions of pounds of explosives out there. But like you said, one in a million."

"And with the lack of evidence," Roz said, "we'll probably never know for sure."

"Consummate Catch also does commercial fishing, right?"

"Right," she said, turning onto A1A.

"So maybe they had a fishing net out there," Alden said.

"And didn't tell their own guide about it?"

"Stuff happens," he said. "Why don't we check them out? I mean really check them out. You're not busy this afternoon, are you?"

Roz pondered the idea as they neared the restaurant. "If this means figuring out why someone is shooting at us, then this is the priority. Besides, I'm going to have a lot more energy after I mainstream a burrito and some soda."

Alden laughed. "You sure you don't want a margarita?"

"You trying to get me drunk?"

"Of course."

Roz couldn't help grinning. "Ask again at dinner."

ALDEN AND ROZ each discreetly left the table during lunch to make phone calls to their respective papers, and together they agreed to wait a day before publishing anything new online about the Bellamy case. Besides, Alden thought, they didn't have anything new anyway, not really. His own attempts to get a comment from Mysty Wellington had been rebuffed, as he knew they would be, but he could be a persistent jerk when he wanted to be, and he'd keep trying. Or maybe get Kat to take a crack at it. Celebrities practically competed to talk with her after her kid-glove treatment of a lovestruck movie director who proposed to—then cast in a film—an obscure European princess he'd met at Lunaria Lodge.

After last night's simmering heat, Roz was all cool business this morning. He'd tried to mirror her attitude for the sake of his own sanity, but to his alarm, the more she resisted his charms, the more fired up he was to break through the ice.

She seemed to warm up to him through lunch and into the afternoon, when they worked together to get as much information as they could on Consummate Catch and its president, Peter Verret. Using Roz's laptop and the wi-fi at the Mosquito County courthouse on the mainland, they found some of the information online. Other documents they had to request from county officials. By late afternoon, when they'd moved on to a table amid the stacks at the Bohemia Public Library, they had compiled an interesting dossier.

For one thing, Peter Verret was making serious money. While they couldn't find records that spoke to how much his company pulled in, they saw how he lived. Property records showed he had large, lavish homes in Sarasota, Bohemia Beach, Marathon in the Keys, and even the chichi Saturn Shores neighborhood of Comet Cove. Locally, he was frequently seen at charity events presenting large checks.

More interesting to Alden was that Verret had a criminal record. In his early twenties, he'd spent time in prison for being caught with drugs aboard a boat. Since then, he'd expanded his fishing business and kept his nose clean, except for a few speeding tickets—presumably in his Porsche 911 Turbo S, another indicator of his wealth; they'd found a photo of him with it on someone else's social media page.

Verret had no accounts on social media at all. Alden couldn't decide if he was being secretive or simply wise.

They learned from news searches that he was active in promoting green fishing techniques and had volunteered to serve as a consultant to a state law enforcement task force dedicated to eliminating illegal offshore fishing.

The company's website gave them more background, citing, in addition to Consummate Catch's three charters (two now, Alden thought), a commercial fishing fleet of six boats. A photo showed the vessels in dock, their cobalt-blue hulls sharp and distinctive.

"Was that shot at Star Harbor? It'd be hard to miss a blue boat like that," Alden noted as they huddled over the laptop in the library.

"True," Roz said quietly, "but I haven't seen them there. Then again, I don't pay much attention to the commercial fishing operations."

"And they don't look anything like the boat in your photos," Alden said.

"You mean the debris pics?" Roz tapped in a new search. "The charter boats probably have a different color scheme. Look at this. The company has multiple addresses. I bet the one in Bohemia Harbor is for the commercial fishing boats. Or at least some of them."

"Maybe try a satellite view." He helped her find the Indian River Lagoon and then Bohemia Harbor on Google Earth, drilling down to the marina's dark blue water—and what looked like an area with warehouses and a couple of bright blue boats. "There!"

"I suppose we're lucky the satellite happened to catch a couple of his boats at the dock. But can I just say that kind of detail from remote eyes in the sky is terrifying?"

He laughed. "Nothing is private anymore."

"Nothing except Peter Verret's real life. It's hard to come

up with a good theory when we essentially have nothing on this guy. He's Mr. Charity and Mr. Eco. Maybe we're barking up the wrong tree."

"He certainly seems like the classic screwup who made good. But I'm still a little puzzled as to why owning a fishing fleet would make him so much money. The guy lives like a movie star."

"And if anyone knows how movie stars live, it's you," Roz teased. "It is puzzling. Maybe he's just brilliant at investing?"

Alden shook his head. "Do you think that drug charge from way back means anything? Could drugs be involved after all?"

"Why don't we get an eye on his operation and see what we see?"

"*Spy* on him?" he blurted. A nearby librarian shushed him.

A corner of Roz's mouth lifted. "Well, we could find the harbor where his boats are docked, where they unload the fish, and see if there's any unusual activity. Maybe go at night. If I were going to do something naughty, that's when I'd do it."

"Oh, if you're going to do something naughty at night, I definitely want to be there," Alden whispered.

"Alden!" she exclaimed.

The librarian hushed them again.

Alden smiled. "Let's get out of here and grab some dinner."

After consulting their respective restaurant apps, they ended up at a New Orleans-themed restaurant and bar in downtown Bohemia called Nola, with lots of plush decor and a tantalizing cocktail menu.

"God, I really want a Sazerac," Alden said.

"That would knock me right out." Roz put aside the cocktail menu and focused on the food. "But I'd like to come back here some night when we don't have a job to do."

Alden noted the "we" with pleasure. "Let's."

Roz glanced at him with a shy smile before returning to her menu.

Alden scanned his. "Hmm, Duck Two Way. Have you ever tried the three-way?"

Roz shot him a wry look. "I have not."

"Neither have I, alas," he said, and she chuckled.

When the server, a slim woman wearing black and a lot of tattoos, arrived at the table, Alden gave in to temptation and ordered a Sazerac. To his disappointment, Roz said no to alcohol, with the excuse that they were still working.

"You could have a glass of wine. A glass of wine never hurt anybody," Alden said after the server left.

"I want to stay crispy if we're going to play detective this evening," she said. "Besides, I have to drive."

"Promise me you'll drink later."

"When later?"

"After you're done working for the evening."

"I'm always up for wine after I'm done working," she said. "But it could be a long night."

"I hope so," he said softly, and something in her eyes gave him irrational hope that they could pick up where they'd left off last night. Except that getting more involved with her seemed almost cruel, to both of them. She wouldn't want to be with him once she knew just how badly he'd messed up his life. And not just his.

Besides, she was too straight-arrow to put up with his nonsense, no matter how much he tried to do the right thing. Her standards were too high, and he'd given up hope of ever being the kind of person she'd want to spend time with in any meaningful way. So maybe it wouldn't be meaningful, but he still hoped they could spend more time together.

The server dropped off his drink, and he regarded his rival over the cold rocks glass with its single fat ice cube. Roz had become more intoxicating than the cocktail, though it was delicious: the peppery sweetness of good rye whiskey, a kiss of absinthe and a breath of citrus, thanks to the lemon twist.

The server returned, and Alden ordered the duck; Roz, the shrimp étouffée. They tried each other's entrees and chatted and laughed, and for a few minutes, he almost forgot his misgivings, forgot that they were working, forgot that much more was at stake. They had to figure out this story before it killed them.

ROZ EYED ALDEN as she sipped her double espresso, now thick and sweet with a couple of packets of raw sugar. She felt nervous about how the evening would go—not the stakeout, so much, though that should make her nervous. No, she thought about more. About whether she wanted more from this man, so cool and funny on the surface, so—something else beneath. Conflicted. Tense and protective and, she had no doubt, passionate. It seemed like everything he did was about hiding who he really was.

"It felt weird today, doing old-fashioned journalism again," Alden said over his end-of-the-meal coffee, which had followed a second cocktail.

"I thought you said what you do is journalism."

"It is, but I play a little fast and loose with the rules sometimes to get what I want."

"That's fine until someone gets hurt," she said.

Alden didn't say anything, just blew on his steaming coffee.

"What is it?" she asked.

He met her gaze. His gray eyes were cloudy. "Sometimes the rules get you into trouble, too."

"If you follow the rules, you never have regrets," Roz said. "I've missed some stories because of ethical choices, and I don't regret it."

"Then you're a better man than I," he said.

"Don't be cryptic, Alden."

"I thought women liked men to be cryptic."

"I don't," she said. He looked as if he was in pain. She wanted to know why. "You told me you screwed up once. Is that what you're talking about?"

"I've screwed up many, many times."

"That's why we run corrections when we have to. Account-ability."

He let out a dry laugh. "Corrections can only do so much when the screwup is the big screwup to screw up all screwups."

She cocked her head in question. "This is what you were talking about on the beach, isn't it?"

He put down the coffee. "I suppose I need to tell you."

"You need to?"

"So I can see whether you ever want to talk to me again."

God, it couldn't be that bad, could it? But he had a haunted look, and it gave her chills.

"I'll talk to you," Roz said. "Tell me."

Alden shook his head, and she thought that was it. Then, after a full minute had ticked by, he stared into his coffee and started talking.

"Once upon a time, a boy lived an enchanted existence in upstate New York. He was an annoying little rich kid, as you'd once surmised, but he wanted to prove he was more than his private school education. So he went to college to study jour-nalism and change the world." Alden took a sip of coffee and resumed staring into his cup. "He got a job at a small-town paper. It was an idyllic town, really, until the Toyman came.

The Toyman wore a clown costume and kidnapped little kids."

"He *what?* Is this for real? Not that novel you're writing?"

"Sounds like a horror movie, doesn't it? Only it was real."

"My God. Did he—did he kill them?" Roz swallowed, dreading the answer.

"He had a tea party with the first child, then took her little scarf. Exactly three hours after he kidnapped her, he let her go, giving her a new toy to take home. He followed the same pattern as he continued. After playing a game with the next child, he took socks and shoes from the boy before he let him go—six hours later. The kids said he didn't touch them in a bad way. In fact, he talked them into getting into his van, and they were so innocent they didn't know any better. So small." Alden's voice cracked, then he took a breath. "Obviously, afterward, they were scared and freaked out. And we all had the feeling it was going to get worse."

Roz wasn't sure she wanted to ask. "It got worse?"

"He abducted a little girl on Halloween who wore a vampire costume and asked for her fake fangs after making her watch a vampire movie with him. He gave her candy and popcorn and filmed her when she fell asleep. He had the nerve to send the video to the cops."

"Creepy. He released her?"

"After nine hours. And he gave her two presents. One he told her to give to the police."

"Bold." Roz scowled.

"Yeah. And sick." Alden's face was somber. "The child got a doll. The 'gift' for the police was a toy clock with the hands set to midnight and a note. It said, 'Dreadful dead of dark midnight.'"

"That—that's horrifying." Roz's mind churned. "He was

clearly escalating. Three hours, six hours, nine ... twelve? And twelve meant death? He was going to kill his next victim?"

"That's what we thought. Though the quote is from Shakespeare, a poem about a different kind of assault. Either way, horrible connotations. No one wanted to risk it happening again."

Roz shivered. "Every parent in town must've been terrified."

"The whole town was basically on lockdown," Alden agreed. "Forensics got nothing from the toys. And then I started getting the emails."

"You? How?"

"I was a young reporter at the local paper, ambitious, dying to get into a big city, really get into the game. And here, this insane crime story fell into my lap. A man wrote me an email saying he had inside information on the bad guy. My source, let's call him Nut Job, and his wife had a day-care. Nut Job's brother was a beloved city councilman who used to help them with maintenance and such. Nut Job pointed out that all of the children who were abducted attended that day care. And Nut Job said he had evidence that his brother, the councilman, was the guy. He'd give it all to me if I protected his identity. He started feeding me information about the councilman. The fact that my chosen suspect had a sex-crime conviction looked really bad on paper, but the crime was a teen prank, mooning a rival team in college. Then Nut Job told me about his brother's contact with the kids, about the toys the man bought for the day-care—he pointed out that every child was released with a new toy." Alden paused again, and his desolate expression almost broke Roz's heart.

"I was willing to protect my source," he said. "I assured my editor that I knew what I was doing, that I trusted Nut

Job. I started to write stories that reiterated the scary crimes, with a dollop of circumstantial evidence and coincidence based on what Nut Job told me. Fed by fear and innuendo, the public used those stories to make the councilman's life a living hell."

"But if he was guilty—" Roz said.

"That's just it. After weeks of these stories, the councilman was shouted out of a town meeting. He lost his business. He tried to kill himself, which probably made him look even more guilty. His wife filed for divorce. One of the victims even said she recognized the councilman's voice when she saw him on TV. Of course, the day-care closed once I wrote about the connection, and Nut Job scolded me for that since it was his business. I started to wonder how Nut Job knew so much about the crimes. I had promised to protect his identity as my anonymous source—"

"Which we do."

"—and I was so reluctant to give up the gravy train. These stories were making bank for the paper. For my reputation. But as much as the councilman was brought in for questioning, as much as his life was ripped apart, the cops never had enough evidence to arrest him. Meanwhile, Nut Job told me he thought the Toyman would act again soon.

"I finally realized that something didn't feel right about his information," Alden continued, "and after agonizing over my promise to keep him anonymous, I went to the police with my suspicions. Based on what I told them, they did a stakeout and caught the perp trying to take another kid. Surprise, surprise. The kidnapper was the councilman's brother—Nut Job— who'd borrowed the councilman's car to further implicate him."

"Oh, God." Roz's stomach clenched, imagining what Alden

had gone through. What the councilman and the parents and the children had suffered, too.

Alden's smile was brittle. "I think he wanted to get caught, partly to show how he'd fooled everybody, including me. We published a huge front-page story—it was essentially the biggest effing retraction you've ever seen, underscoring the councilman's innocence. But it was really too late. Any whisper of that kind of crime around anyone, and you're tainted for life. Some people wondered if the councilman had conspired with his Nut Job brother. But Nut Job was the sicko, and the councilman paid the price. He's probably still paying the price."

Alden swirled his cup. "I was dressed down by my editor," he continued. "He questioned my judgment—as if I weren't questioning my own judgment. I had done what I thought I was supposed to do. You make a promise to an anonymous source, you keep that promise. Only in this case, keeping that promise meant misery and injustice. It *almost* meant more victims." Alden stopped talking, his face contorted with anguish. In a moment, she saw him get ahold of himself, saw the cool facade return.

"You were inexperienced. You couldn't have known," Roz said.

"If I'd been less freaking ambitious, if I'd questioned this guy even a little, I would have been more cautious. You don't take an anonymous source's dish just because they're offering. You have to figure out their agenda. If I'd thought about it, I wouldn't have made any promises. And I wouldn't have ruined a life."

"You did what you could to fix it. You did the right thing. You even got the bad guy caught. Saved a life."

"But with so much wreckage." Alden made it sound like a

joke, but she heard the pain in his voice. "There was a libel suit from the councilman. The paper could have proved it didn't act with malice. I'd carefully worded the stories. But they agreed on a modest settlement to try to right the wrong. That was a good paper. "

Roz offered him an ironic smile. "And you never got the punishment you thought you deserved?"

His laugh was bitter. "That's one way to put it."

"And you left newspapers."

"And went to the tabloids, where what we were writing about didn't really matter, and how I got the information didn't matter, either. I stayed away from stories that would really hurt anybody, but I got good at digging up the details people loved to read. Some of them were hurtful, I guess, but those were all a matter of public record—well-hidden arrest reports, surveillance video, that kind of thing. No one got called out who didn't deserve it. That's what I told myself."

Roz wanted to reach for him but sensed that the slightest touch might crack the fragile shell that was holding him together right now.

"And then you came to Comet Cove?" she asked.

"The tabloid owner started *The Beacon* and thought I'd be a great asset for its mission: amusing gossip. Small-town features. Nothing heavy. I was ready to get out of the dirt business, so I came here."

"And now we're looking into a heavy, dirty story about an exploding movie star."

"Exactly." His smile was half real, half mask. She reached out and covered his hand with hers. He looked down for a moment as if he didn't know how to process her touch, and then he flipped his hand over and clasped hers and squeezed it tight.

They sat for a minute or two like that, not talking, drinking their coffee, until the cups were empty and he let go.

"Ready to play *Dragnet?*" Alden asked, his mocking smile back in place.

"*This is the city*," she intoned, playing along. "Bohemia, Florida ..."

"Come on, Girl Friday," he said, and they paid and left the restaurant.

chapter
## **twenty-one**

SO MAYBE HE shouldn't have had the second drink. It made him maudlin and confessional, and at the advanced age of thirty-four, he should know better. But Alden felt a strange, exhausted relief at having told Roz about the story that would always haunt him.

He watched her as they walked back toward where she'd parked in a downtown Bohemia lot near the train tracks, not far from the harbor home of Consummate Catch. It was dark now, and the town's decorative streetlights cast spangles in her hair and sculpted the soft angles of her face with shadows.

She'd taken his hand at the table, but that was just sympathy, he was sure. Or pity. He hated pity. He'd almost prefer that she despise him.

He wanted her to want him, not pity him. To want him in spite of everything.

"Do you think we should try to park closer?" Roz asked, oblivious to his thoughts.

He glanced at the map app on his phone. "Actually, I think you're in a good spot, camouflaged by tourists and partiers, close enough to the water. And more bars, if we want another drink." He pointed at The Junction Box. "That's a good one."

She chuckled. "We're working. I just want to be sure we can walk to where we need to be and get back to the car in a hurry if we have to."

"This should be perfect." They'd reached the parking lot.

Roz locked her bag in the car and gave her keys to Alden. "No pockets," she said apologetically.

They walked downhill toward the harbor, away from the buzz of happy people having a good time on the main drag. What a concept, he thought—not working on a Friday night.

There were a few restaurants and bars down here by the water, too, taking advantage of the views, but fewer pedestrians. Roz and Alden strolled along the walkway around the harbor, trying to look touristy as they scanned the yachts and sailboats dominating the slips. Ahead of them was a cluster of duller-looking buildings that faced the water.

"Blue boats," Roz murmured.

"That's got to be it."

As they got closer, Roz pointed to a sign over a door on one of the industrial buildings that backed up to the docks: *Consummate Catch Fishing & Charters.*

Beyond it, a few of Consummate's commercial fishing boats were docked, their distinctive blue color notable even in the patchy artificial light. Alongside them were a couple of smaller red-and-white vessels that must have been the charter boats.

"So they run charters out of here and Comet Cove," Alden noted.

"We shouldn't stay here," Roz said. They were standing dockside, right outside the industrial building. "We'll be seen."

"We can hang out near the pleasure boats. Looks like there

are more of them in the slips beyond the warehouses. We can sit on the dock next to one of them and pretend we're tourists or sailors."

"Tourist is a role I can play," she said. "Sailor, not so much."

They stood for a moment, listening. Her long dress caught the breeze and swirled dramatically around her legs. He was so distracted, he almost didn't hear the voices behind them.

*"Alden,"* Roz whispered.

Alden grabbed her hand and started walking. He liked the feel of her hand in his, even if he was just playing a role.

She looked up at him in surprise as she kept up, ignoring the people walking behind them.

"We're tourists," he explained, "having a romantic evening."

A corner of her mouth turned up, but she didn't say anything, just focused straight ahead as they walked past the closed doors of the big Consummate Catch building and farther down the docks, toward the privately owned boats. They passed a couple of rows of slips and sat in the middle of a dock, a spot mostly shielded by a darkened yacht. The people they'd heard had walked another way, and now no one was in sight.

"Seems pretty quiet," Roz said.

"Too quiet," Alden agreed with faux drama.

She snickered. "I guess it's too early to call it a night. We just got here. But my patience with wild goose chases is not high."

"We can't call it a wild goose chase until we're completely bored, our butts hurt from sitting on these planks, and we have to pee."

"What if my butt already hurts?"

Alden smiled. "You can sit on my lap."

"I'm feeling better already," Roz said.

"How's this?" He got up and moved across the dock, sat and leaned against a post. "Lean against me and relax. We'll still have a good view, and we won't look like we're having a foodless picnic."

She watched him from the middle of the dock for a moment before she got up and sat next to him. She spread her skirt around her and rested against him.

Alden smelled jasmine and, trying to subdue his craving, casually draped an arm over her shoulders.

"This would be more convincing with champagne," she said idly.

"Maybe another night." The moon was high and getting fat, though mostly obscured by scudding clouds. "The moon'll be full in a couple of days. We can get some champagne and go howling."

"If you're a werewolf, I'm drawing the line at working with you," Roz said.

"What about a wolf?"

She looked up into his grin. "You like people to think that, don't you?"

"That I'm a wolf? Appearances aren't always deceiving."

"There's more to you, and for some reason, you don't want people to know it."

Alden shifted, uncomfortable with her insight but craving it just the same. He held her a little more tightly and listened to the creaking of the boats and the slosh of the waves.

"What a cozy stakeout," Roz said softly after a few minutes.

"Except for the lack of champagne."

"True."

"We could go on a booze run," he said.

She giggled and smacked his knee. He felt a surge of sensation a little further north.

"Does the FBI go on booze runs?" she asked.

"They have a guy for that, I'm pretty sure. Though mostly it's doughnut runs."

Roz chuckled again. "We need an intern."

"I understand the *Courier* can use all the free help it can get," he agreed.

"Shut up," she said, elbowing him.

"You need to stop abusing me, or I'll file a police report with that forbidding Officer Byrd. She looked ready to arrest you this morning."

"I think you like it when I abuse you," Roz teased.

"You have a point. Just being with you is torture. Torture me some more."

"Ha! That wasn't torture."

"Please. You're giving me ideas." He pulled her closer and kissed her neck. And she didn't seem upset at all.

ALDEN'S KISS didn't upset Roz, not at all, probably because this was the kind of attention she'd been craving all day, even as she realized how unwise it was. But it had been so, well, fun —not to mention comfortable and companionable—to spend her day with Alden in a common pursuit. And then so difficult to hear him tell his story of failure and to know he still carried that pain with him, under all the arrogance and jokes. His tale made her want to save him from his core of anguish and darkness, a task that was almost certainly beyond her power.

She should've pushed him away, but she liked the feel of him as he cupped her chin and gently turned her face toward his. In the half light, his handsome face looked serious in a whole different way from before.

"This is nice and warm," Roz said, looking into his eyes, questioning. The breeze lofted her long hair and tried to lift her skirt.

"You call it nice. I still call it torture," Alden whispered. He slipped his hand into her hair, pulled her close and lowered his mouth onto hers.

His possession was as electric as the night, which was alive with the sound of the wind, the scent of the salty water and of him, that clean scent that made her think of crisp, white shirts and fresh air. She opened her mouth to his hungry tongue, let a whimper escape as his strong hand pressed against her back. Her body almost vibrated with the sensations overwhelming her.

*Vibration. Noise.*

She pushed a hand against his chest, breaking the spell. "Do you hear that?" she asked.

"All I hear is the blood rushing in my ears."

"Then listen." She pressed a finger against his lips and tried to ignore how soft they were. "A motor." Was it a boat?

"It's just a truck," Alden said. He gasped as Roz rolled away from him and looked in the direction of their quarry.

"I think it's going to Consummate Catch," she whispered. "Let's check it out."

"This really is torture," he moaned as he climbed to his feet and smoothed his hair and clothes.

"Shhh. Let's go up behind these other buildings and circle back around." She took his hand and tugged him across and off the docks, then along an alley behind a cluster of businesses situated across the access road from Consummate Catch.

This neighborhood was disorienting. The buildings and

paved lots were a jumble as they stacked up against the irregular waterline. She had no idea how to get back to the car from here and hoped they wouldn't have to leave in a hurry.

"Stop," Alden said, calm and collected again, halting her before she could plunge forward into the next parking lot. "We don't want to be seen."

"But I can't see *them*," Roz said, impatient. From behind this building, they had no view at all of Consummate Catch. "Let me peek." Before he could stop her, she popped her head around the corner, did a quick reconnaissance and leaned back. "There's a truck unloading stuff into their warehouse, it looks like. It's backed up to the door. I saw someone pull a box out."

"A box of what? Bananas? Coke? Cocktail parasols?"

"I don't know. You didn't want me to be seen!"

"Touché," he said with a nod. "How about we just stroll across the parking lot like we belong here and see if we can get a better view?"

"You mean walk right up to them?"

"Hell, no. What if they *are* drug dealers? Let's walk over there." Alden pointed to a clump of trees next to a closed cafe across the parking lot from them but still less than fifty yards from Consummate Catch. It was fairly dark, and the moon was playing hide-and-seek with the clouds. If they could get to the bushes without being seen, they'd have a decent observation point.

"Should we run?" Roz asked.

"No. We're out for a romantic stroll, remember?" Alden wrapped an arm around her shoulders and guided her in the direction of the trees.

Nervous, Roz slipped her arm around his waist and tried to pick up their pace.

"Women, always wanting to lead the dance," Alden teased.

"Relax." He leaned over her and planted a sweet kiss on her mouth. "That was for authenticity," he whispered.

Buoyed by the kiss, Roz glanced over at the Consummate building. There were a few workers in sight, moving around the gray truck's back end, which faced the open bay door of the warehouse.

Abruptly, the dark lot that separated the warehouse from the reporters lit up like snow.

"And I used to think the moon was romantic," Alden hissed, this time pushing her toward the trees.

They sprinted the last ten yards under the moonlight, stopped behind the clump of landscaping and took a gander. As far as she could tell, they hadn't been spotted. At least, no one had come out to chase them.

The mischievous moon slipped back behind the clouds, and the silver light that had threatened to expose them faded away.

After a few minutes of heavy breathing that had nothing to do with Alden and much more to do with fear, Roz started to relax and pay more attention to their view. Now they had a much better angle to see into the warehouse. It appeared the workers were simply unloading white boxes from the truck outside and reloading them into the back of a box truck inside the structure.

"That seems pointless," Roz whispered.

"Not if they don't want to connect whatever's in Truck A to wherever Truck B is going," Alden replied. "Or maybe they're just distributing produce or something along with their fish."

"Then why is Truck A unmarked? I can't see all of Truck B, but it's bright blue like the boats. It's branded. And we didn't find anything about a distribution business. What if they *are* transporting drugs? They could put them in the fish truck and move them around, and no one would be the wiser if they avoided inspection."

"Maybe you can order grouper stuffed with cocaine."

"Gross," Roz said.

"Why don't we work our way around and get the license plate of the truck? At least then we can figure out who they are."

"They'll see us!"

"No, they won't," Alden said. "You head out there"—he pointed to where this access road connected to another—"and I'll meet you on the other side of that bait and tackle business. See it?"

"And you're going to do what?" Roz asked nervously.

"Get the license plate. I won't be a minute."

chapter
## twenty-two

ROZ TRIED NOT to panic as Alden started rummaging among the bushes, stuck his hand into the hedge and pulled it out with an "Ow!" He held an empty bottle that, according to its label, once held a third-rate vodka. "You can always count on some bum to throw his empty into the bushes."

"Alden, what are you going to do?" Roz tugged at his arm, trying to instill reason.

"See you on the other side," he said with a smile, tugging his shirt out of his pants. He staggered out into the lot.

"This can't be good," Roz mumbled, slipping into the shadows next to the buildings and trotting toward the access road. She heard singing and looked back over her shoulder to see Alden weaving around on the pavement, pretending to drink from the bottle and warbling a seriously off-key "What Shall We Do With a Drunken Sailor?"

She ran to the protection of another cluster of landscaping, this one across the road from where she'd been and near an intersection. She was out of sight of Consummate Catch but could clearly see Alden as he tripped toward the gray truck.

And then the moon shed its cloudy veil again, shining a spot-light on him.

"Put him in the longboat till he's sober!" Alden bellowed. "Put him in the longboat till he's sober, earl-aye in the morning!"

"Hey, what're you doing there?" a gruff voice came from somewhere behind him.

"You got a drink?" Alden called out, his voice slurred.

"Get out of here before we send you up the crow's nest, you idiot."

"Yo ho ho!" Alden said, changing direction, heading toward Roz. "Put me in bed with the captain's daughter, put me in bed with the captain's daughter, put me in bed with the captain's daughter, earl-aye in the morning!"

She heard distant laughter. They thought he was a joke. Good.

She wasn't laughing by the time he caught up with her. "What the hell was that?" she whispered.

"I thought I made a very convincing drunk."

"Well, you are a journalist."

"We can discuss it later, if you don't mind." Alden pulled her farther into the shadows, pulled out his phone and made a note.

Then they jogged away from the docks, keeping buildings between them and the warehouse. They shifted and turned and turned again, working their way back to the public parking area near the restaurants.

Alden tossed the bottle into a trash can as they got to the lot, then tucked in his shirt. "I suppose you wouldn't want that drink now?"

"I am way too freaked out," Roz said. "Let's wait till we get home."

Alden smiled. "I like the sound of that."

"Drinking or home?"

"Either one. Let's get out of here."

ALDEN ARGUED with Roz as they worked their way out of Bohemia and took the causeway over the lagoon to Bohemia Beach, then turned south on A1A toward Comet Cove. The topic: where she was going to stay the night. He saw only one logical choice, and it wasn't her house.

"They haven't made any more attempts to do anything to me, whoever they are," Roz said.

"Because you've been out of town all day and basically untraceable." Alden wanted her to stay with him, and not just because of an irrational desire to tear her clothes off. "Why not stay with me? You have a cat to feed or something?"

"I could stay with my mom. She has a cat to feed," Roz joked.

"Is she all right?" he asked.

"She was this afternoon when I called."

"Then you might as well stay away. They have to know who your mom is if they looked up the boat registration. If you go there, you could just lead them to her." Perhaps it wasn't fair to bring up her mother, but Roz was too bullheaded for her own good.

Roz sighed as they reached the Comet Cove city limit. "I packed a bag this morning. I could stay at one of the beach hotels. The One Small Step Motel is cheap."

"Oh, lord, don't stay at the Small Step," Alden said. "I see the exterminator parked there a little too often, if you know what I mean."

"I think he's dating the clerk. Anyway, it fits my budget. And it's supposed to be one small step to the beach."

"I love a moon-landing pun as much as the next guy, but come on. Come home with me. Or—I could call Lunaria Lodge and see if they have a vacancy."

"Now that's totally impossible," she said. "I can't afford it."

"I can," he said.

"*The Beacon* pays that well?"

"I have a little money put away." He didn't want to mention his modest share of the family fortune, a fund he rarely tapped. "Just let me call."

"Why not another one of the beach hotels?"

"Because Lunaria has a security staff and it's not as easy to access." Alden got off the phone a minute later. "They have a cottage with your name on it. Actually, my name, in case someone's looking for you."

"This is too generous of you," she said. "I'll drop you off at home, and then I'll go there and hide. But I'll pay you back, I swear."

"No and no. It's in my name, and I'm going with you. Besides, my car is still up there."

"*Alden.*" They reached the bridge and paused at a red light at a busy cross-street on the north side of the inlet.

"*Roz.* You are not prying me from this car until we reach Lunaria Lodge."

She glanced over at him. In her pale eyes, he saw frustration and fear and thanks and a light he didn't recognize, a spark that gave him a hopeful thrill.

"OK," she murmured. "But this doesn't mean you're the boss of me."

He laughed. "Heaven forbid."

Roz rolled forward and up and over the causeway, then

took a left at the other side of the bridge toward Lunaria Lodge.

They parked in the main lot. Alden checked in while Roz got her overnight bag and satchel. He met her in front of the main building where it faced the beach. It was almost midnight, and the clouds had thinned, letting moonlight shimmer on the ocean and weave magical shadows through the tropical foliage of the resort.

Alden smiled at Roz, who looked nervous, and led her down the paver-lined path toward their beachfront cottage.

They let themselves in with the key card. Inside, the building was decked out in a studied boho style. Lamps had gorgeous pastel shades of paper pressed with leaves and flowers, and matching floor lamps looked like big leaves of textured paper stitched together. Really nice paintings by local artists adorned the colorful walls, beachy but not cheesy.

"This place is stunning." Roz dropped her bag by the couch, then wended her way through the sliding doors out to the dark patio and pool, made more private by a screened enclosure lined with tropical plants. Alden followed, and they both took in the view of the glittering ocean.

"This is extravagant," she said. "I thought they had hotel rooms up at the main building?"

"They do, but they're all booked for a wedding. Enjoy it."

"OK." She glanced at him. "Thank you. This is magnificent."

Alden had to agree as he stood back and watched her. She closed her eyes and breathed deeply of the sea air. The wind lifted her thick hair and swirled the long skirt of her outfit around her, its slit revealing her shapely legs as the fabric clung to her curves and wafted in the breeze like a flag.

He stepped up behind her and slipped his arms around her waist.

Roz stiffened, but he just held her close, his front to her back, willing her to relax.

"What are you afraid of?" he whispered in her ear.

"Besides getting shot at?"

"You know what I mean."

She was silent for a few moments, but he felt the rigidity in her muscles ease. "Oh, where do I start?" she said softly. "Failure, for one thing. Falling short of my potential, losing my career."

"I know from experience that it's not the career that matters unless it truly makes you happy."

"Are you happy?" Roz asked.

Alden shifted, not wanting to lose her. "I'm working on it. Are you afraid of me?"

He could barely hear her response. "Maybe I am afraid of taking things further with you," she said. "I know I'm afraid of losing the paper before we can sell it and make my mom comfortable. If I lose to you, I mean if the *Courier* loses to *The Beacon,* then I've failed. So—yes, Alden. I suppose I am afraid of you."

"I think you're afraid of more than your paper folding." He nuzzled her hair. "I want to hear you say 'Yes, Alden' and not be afraid." He pulled her ever so slightly closer. "I'll let you win."

"Why is that so hard to believe?" Roz no doubt meant it sarcastically, but he heard the tremor of doubt in her voice. It fanned the spark of hope inside him into a fire.

Why he wanted her so badly, he couldn't articulate. So much for the writer in him. He only knew that a quality inside her spoke to the same sensibility in him. He craved her sureness and her strength. More to the point, he craved *her*, every stubborn, voluptuous, forbidden inch of her.

"Believe me," Alden said. "I need you—to believe me. To believe *in* me."

The wind rose. Alden felt a change in her body as her breathing quickened.

"Don't you ever just want to let go of all your rules? Your fears?" He kissed her neck, and she melded against him. "Don't worry, Roz. I'll catch you if you slip off your white unicorn."

She chuckled softly. "Alden ... this is, like, the bad idea to end all bad ideas."

"I think it's brilliant," he murmured, kissing her under her ear.

She made a soft sound, not quite a sigh. "How are we ever going to go back to hating each other?" she asked, tilting her head to give him better access.

"We'll figure out a way, I'm sure." Alden smiled into her neck, then nipped the lobe of her ear. He turned her to face him, wrapped her up in his arms and slanted his mouth across hers. She opened to him slowly, and he savored the sweet unfurling of her desire, the petals of a flower revealing itself, her jasmine scent a drug to his senses. But as soon as he moved his hands to her hips, she pushed him away.

"Do I have to beg?" he joked, then knelt before her.

"Oh!" She looked down at him with luminous eyes. As the wind lifted her long skirt, he leaned in and kissed one knee, still encased in the tights. She giggled.

He stood with a grin. "I liked the view from down there with your skirt flying around my head. *Blow, blow, thou winter wind, Thou art not so unkind.*"

"Shakespeare? That seems awfully romantic for you, Alden."

"The rest of the speech is pretty cynical, actually. Not that I meant it that way." He pulled her into an embrace, a big, warm hug. He could do those, too, even when he wanted more. "You said you wanted wine? I had them deliver some before we arrived."

"Red?"

"And white. And champagne. Just to be safe."

She snorted. "Doesn't sound very safe to me."

"Is safe what you really want?" He released her, held her at arm's distance, searching her eyes for what felt like forever.

"Usually," she finally said. "But not tonight."

# twenty-three

WHEN ROZ AWOKE, it took her a full minute to realize where she was. She stretched against the decadent bedding of the Lunaria resort, rolled onto her back and found herself alone as morning light filtered into the room.

But she hadn't been alone last night.

The birds chirping and watery sounds filtering through the windows were relaxing and not terribly conducive to facing reality. And reality had just taken a turn.

"Hmmm." She glanced at the clock—9:45 a.m., making it an indulgent sleep for her. She stared up at the ceiling, turning warm as she remembered every moment of her night with Alden.

What should she call it? A hookup? She didn't go for hookups. Lovemaking? As a wordsmith, she wasn't sure that was the right term, either. Were they headed down a road toward love? Was that even possible? Maybe their encounter was more like the kind of liaison co-workers had when chemistry took over. Not that she'd ever experienced anything like this. Or maybe it was the kind of sex people had when they thought they were going to die.

Now, that wasn't a pleasant thought. And besides, she had feelings she couldn't dismiss as base hormonal reactions. Yes, Alden was attractive—who was she kidding, *incredibly* attractive—but she found herself admiring much more about him. His humor. His cleverness. His wild persistence. His scars and his morality, which he held so closely, masked by cynicism and wit. And his surprising tenderness, so sweet after his delicious possession of her.

But now, where the heck was he? Out getting the story?

*I'll let you win,* he'd said.

Ha. Not that she'd ever want anyone to let her win at anything.

It was Saturday. Her staff had the weekend off, as a rule. If there was a story that absolutely had to get online, she generally handled it, but it was almost always a down day. Without other pressures, she could focus on the Boyd Bellamy story. She ran over the to-do list in her mind, then slipped out of bed, donned the fluffy white robe she found in the closet, and went to look for her overnight bag.

She was halted in the living room by the sound of a splash and wandered to the sliding doors.

Alden was swimming laps in the pool. Naked.

*Holy pecs.* He was even more gorgeous in daytime. Sunlight glinted off his tan, wet skin, and his thick, dark hair somehow seemed even more luxuriant when he stopped and stood, chest-deep in the water, and ran his hands through it, drips flying. Was he doing this just to torment her? To remind her of how far she'd—they'd gone?

She didn't need to be reminded, but she didn't mind looking.

Maybe he sensed her standing there, because he looked up toward the sliding doors. Could he see her?

His slow smile said yes. Like a a shot of tequila, it made her forget that her reckless night would almost certainly result in a hell of a hangover. But oh, it felt so good.

She kicked herself for the girly thrill he gave her. Especially when he climbed out of the pool, wrapped a towel around his waist and walked toward her.

Roz opened the door for him.

"Good morning," he said.

"Good morning." She couldn't help scanning him again. "Alden, don't let this go to your head, but you're not half bad-looking."

He grinned. "Thanks. Nice robe."

"Isn't it? I found it in the closet."

"Want me to take it off?"

She quelled a sigh. "I think maybe we should focus on figuring out a few things this morning."

"Having regrets?"

"I'm talking about the story."

"Of course." He nodded. "I can switch to business mode."

"Not in that towel, you can't." Freaking distracting, that towel.

"If you insist," he said, pulling off the towel and dropping it to the floor.

"Th—that's not what I meant!" she stammered.

He grinned again and pulled her to him with one arm, laying a crushed-velvet kiss on her lips that made her want to melt into a puddle. After a few indulgent seconds, Roz pushed him away and tried to catch her breath. "We have to work. And you—you have to put your pants on."

"You sure?" he teased, noting her roving eyes.

"Yes? Yes!" She forced herself to look up at his face. "Holy hole in a doughnut, Alden. I'm going to take a shower. Alone," she said as he opened his mouth. "And then maybe we can get something done. Or—go back to our offices."

"I've booked the cottage for tonight, too." He casually secured the towel back around his waist. "We could work here."

"OK." Why did she feel so shy? "I'll be right back."

Roz found her bag—with the clothes she'd discarded last night neatly folded on top of it—and took it to the bedroom to get ready for the day.

She emerged wearing jeans and a white blouse over a white tank top with her favorite freshwater pearl earrings and matching necklace. Her shoes were practical—black slip-ons with a low heel, complemented by sky-blue socks for color— and now she felt more like herself, ready to take care of business.

Alden had transformed, too, into an azure-blue button-up shirt, rolled up at the sleeves, and weathered black jeans. He was seated on a couch facing the coffee table, which held his laptop and a tempting platter of bagels, along with plates and silverware.

Roz frowned. "Where'd you get those clothes?"

"I woke up a lot earlier than you, and since my car was already here, I drove home and packed a bag."

"But not a swimsuit," she noted with irony.

"I couldn't resist the private pool. Did you really mind?" He grinned. "Got my laptop, too."

She wondered what else he'd been up to. "Any news?" she probed as she sat down and popped open her laptop, cranking it up.

He chuckled. "Don't worry. I'm not far ahead of you. At least I brought you breakfast. Cream cheese is in the card- board container."

Roz picked out a cinnamon raisin bagel and slathered cream cheese on it as he watched with amusement.

"So," Alden said, "our friend Mysty Wellington has made a wedding announcement in *Star Style* magazine. It's on their website."

"What? She's marrying her girlfriend?" Roz asked around a bite of bagel.

"It appears so."

"Does she say where?"

"Interestingly, Florida."

"Hmm," Roz said. "Wonder if she's just trying to make everybody forget her date with her ex."

"That's my guess. My story about the carriage ride was picked up all over the place. And if she's getting married in Florida, especially if she's getting married here in Comet Cove, she might let everyone conclude that was really why she was in the area—to get married here. Maybe she wanted the carriage ride to seem like a sideshow, though it wasn't mentioned in the short piece about the wedding. Maybe she wanted to break the news to Boyd or something, or maybe that's what she wants everyone to think."

"Do you think her plans were more nefarious?" Roz asked.

"Boyd did die in a boat explosion. They could've met before that and we just don't know about it. Maybe she engineered the explosion, too."

"How could she do that?"

"What, now you want my theory to make sense?" Alden joked. "Actually, I asked around about Consummate Catch's fishing guide—made a few phone calls to his neighbors and tracked down a couple of friends. As far as they knew, he had no connection to Mysty."

Well, Alden had been busy. "This is all so bizarre," Roz said. "I just don't know where she fits into all this."

"Me either." Alden stood. "Want some OJ? I have some in the fridge. The fresh-squeezed stuff."

"Oh, yes, please." Roz offered him a genuine smile. This was so comfortable. Weird, but comfortable.

He returned with two glasses of liquid ambrosia, and they talked over the possibilities. Roz called Sirenia's catering department, and the manager who answered said they were too crazed with today's wedding to talk to her but wouldn't confirm Mysty's wedding even if they were catering it, citing privacy issues. Alden went another route, searching Mosquito County wedding licenses online.

"Bingo." He sounded triumphant. "It doesn't say where they're getting married, but the fact that they got the license in this county suggests that, at the very least, they plan to get married in the area. And why not at Lunaria Lodge?"

"Could be Bohemia Beach. You don't know."

"Either way, I need to get an item online about that." He shot a look at her. "You don't mind?"

"Please," Roz said, waving him off. "Unless I confirm it's in Comet Cove or get more context, I'm not interested. I like facts with my gossip."

"OK," he said. "I know this is strange, us working on the same story, but I was serious about not stepping on your toes."

"Do what you have to do, Alden," Roz said, reminding herself that, if they had a real conflict, the *Courier* had to come first.

He granted her a half smile that gave him an irresistible dimple and made his gray eyes sparkle, and then he set about typing up his item while she called Duke.

"Deputy Dawson," he answered his phone.

"Hey, it's Roz."

"About time you called me. Are you OK?"

"Yes, fine," she said, surprised by the concern in his voice. "So you heard about my little incident?"

"Incidents, you mean. We've been keeping an eye out, but we haven't noted any unusual activity, and I've run some extra patrols by your place. Looks like no one's home? And you're not at your mom's, I take it."

There was more than professional curiosity in his voice. "I found a safe place to stay temporarily," she said, not wanting to reveal more. "Have you guys had any luck on that partial plate?"

"The one the pretty boy got from the attack car?" Duke's tone made Roz laugh, and Alden raised an eyebrow at her. "The first few letters matched a report of a stolen plate in Orlando a few days ago," Duke continued. "Doesn't give us much to go on."

"No, it sure doesn't," Roz said in frustration. "Look, Duke, if I asked you to look up another plate, would you be willing?"

He paused. "What's the deal?"

She didn't see any reason not to tell him. "You know that company that runs the fishing charter whose boat blew up? The plate was on a truck that was parked there when I went to have a look at the building. No markings. I just wanted to see who owned it."

"Well, since you could just go online and pay somebody twenty bucks for the same information, I suppose I could do it," Duke said good-humoredly.

"Want twenty bucks?"

He laughed. "No, thanks. That's crossing the line. But I'm still up for ice cream one day. I'll give you a call when I get some info."

"Thanks, Duke. You're the best." She gave him the plate number Alden had connived to get the night before.

"Be careful. Let me know if you see anything unusual."

"Will do. Talk to you later." She disconnected the call and took a sip of her orange juice.

Alden had stopped typing and was looking at her. "So how's good ol' Duke?"

She couldn't help goading him. "He called you a pretty boy."

"Did he now? I didn't think I was the one he was interested in."

Roz laughed out loud. "I think you're safe. He's going to look up the license plate for us."

"You mean for *you*. I noticed I wasn't mentioned."

"We each have our ways," Roz said with a smile.

"I like your way."

"Yours is pretty nice, too."

Alden slid closer to her on the couch and clasped the back of her neck, pulling her in for a slow, searing kiss.

Her smartphone burst into its jarring ringtone, the vibrating bell of an analog phone.

She broke off the kiss with a gasp. "Yeesh."

Alden smiled and went back to tapping on his computer as she answered it.

"Roz Melander."

"It's Duke. Interesting character owns your truck."

"Who?" She tried not to sound winded as she prepared to type into the notes file open on her laptop.

"Company run by Galeno Z. Garza," he said, spelling the name for her. "He was once arrested on charges of trafficking cocaine, but he beat the rap. Lawyer got him off on an illegal search. He's kept out of trouble for a while. Or at least, there's been no indication he's still in the drug business, based on police records."

"Is his company based in Comet Cove or Bohemia?"

"Bohemia. Seguro Trucking. That's all I know."

"That's fabulous, Duke. I definitely owe you an ice cream now," Roz said.

"At least one, since you owe me twenty bucks' worth." Duke chuckled at his own joke. "Call me if you need me, and don't do anything foolish. This guy's a heavy hitter or was at one time."

"You rock. Thanks. Bye."

Alden eyed her suspiciously as she set down her phone.

"If you owe anyone an ice cream, it's me," he said.

She laughed. "You have a point. Consider this an IOU. I'll buy you one, too."

chapter
## twenty-four

ALDEN GOT a kick out of watching Roz work.

Of course, he'd rather do more than work with her, but he realized they had priorities. The sooner they figured out who was threatening Roz, the easier it would be to think about other things. Like that plush pink mouth as she absently chewed on the end of a black plastic pen while she typed on her laptop, doing online research.

Besides, his worry for her had grown to such a point that this morning, he'd quietly talked to the security company Deputy Boyd recommended about posting a stealthy bodyguard to keep an eye on her whenever she ventured out alone. She'd probably be furious at the surveillance, but she didn't need to know, and if his covert action saved her life, the risk of annoying her was worth it.

"So tell me what Officer Duke told you about the truck," Alden said. "Unless you need the scoop."

"Knowing who owned a truck is not a scoop. And you got the plate number." Roz filled him in on the details.

"So a known drug dealer is transferring stuff from his truck to a truck at Consummate Catch," Alden said.

"I believe so. It's just unclear what that 'stuff' is."

"Have you searched to see if this Garza has a connection with Verret?"

"That's what's interesting," Roz said, scrolling through pages on her computer. "The only thing they have in common is a nonprofit that promotes ocean conservation, advocates clean water, fights overfishing, that sort of thing. It sounds pretty innocent."

"But where's the fun in that?" Alden said, and she chuckled. "We didn't see much at the fish place. Maybe we should drop by the trucking company."

Roz regarded him warily. "You have to promise me you won't pretend to be a drunk and try to get yourself killed again."

"Aw, Ms. Melander, does that mean you care?"

"Hmph. I just don't want to blow the story, is all."

Alden enjoyed her obvious denial. "What if I were genuinely drunk? Would that be better?"

"More authentic but not necessarily better."

"I'll promise not to pose as a drunkard. However, if I am drunk, all bets are off."

"Then I'll try to keep you sober at lunch," Roz said.

"As much as I like the idea of you taking me out to lunch, I like the idea even better of having lunch here."

Was it his imagination, or did she turn just a bit pink? "We can't dilly-dally, Alden."

"I just wanted to dally." The teasing wasn't working, and Alden gave in, as he knew he must. "OK, we'll have lunch and see what we can see at Seguro Trucking."

"Thank you," Roz said. "But let's approach more cautiously this time."

"It doesn't have to be all cloak and dagger," he said. "We'll go in the daylight and check it out. We'll look like a couple of tourists."

"Touring Bohemia's industrial district?"

"We'll be lost tourists."

Two hours later, after mostly fruitless online research, Alden drove Roz north over the inlet bridge in his car, with the top down. It was impossible not to enjoy the sunny, cool weather, the kind of perfect Florida day that got tourists to the beaches, anglers on the water and convertible drivers on the road.

"We'll *have* to pose as tourists in this red Miata," she said to him over the roar of the wind as they cruised north. "It's not exactly subtle."

"But don't you love it?" Alden said, momentarily happy in his Ray-Bans, with Roz beside him in her cute, cheap sunglasses. She'd put her hair up in a twist, but escaped strands flew all over the place, lending her an air of enchanting disarray. He focused on the carefree moment and tried not to think about this story's grim beginning and unknown end.

To the east, the ocean twinkled, crystalline turquoise this morning. It was easy to forget that somewhere out there, it hid unexploded bombs, bad guys with guns, and erstwhile movie stars.

They stopped in Bohemia Beach, found an oceanfront seafood place packed with tourists and sat on the outside deck. Over delicious fresh mahi sandwiches, they spent a leisurely hour and a half chatting about things that had nothing to do with the story. Alden indulged in just one beer, lest he worry Roz, and quizzed her about her path to newspapers (growing up with the *Courier*, ink in her veins; university for journalism; a medium-size paper in North Carolina; and then the smaller, feisty paper in Baltimore).

"You're lucky to be so close to your family," Alden said. "Or to have a family worth being close to."

"Except after Mom, I'm the only one left. You're not close to yours?" She sipped her iced tea, as relaxed as he'd ever seen her.

"They hated me going into journalism. My father, especially. He wanted me to be a lawyer like him. Once they got a whiff of my cascading failures, they didn't go out of their way to contact me."

"And have you contacted them?"

"Rarely," Alden said, annoyed that the question made him defensive. "There's only so much disapproval I can take. They always know where I am. I let them know about the Comet Cove job. They have a vacation home just up the coast in Cocoa Beach. If they want to see me, they can call anytime." And they hadn't yet, he thought. Alden took a sip of his beer and tried to calm himself. He never liked talking about his family. "As families go, I'm better off without them."

"That's too bad," Roz said, and her sympathy made him feel worse. "Any siblings?"

"Fortunately, I have a younger brother who has outstripped me in popularity by becoming a lawyer like dear old dad. He and the wife have produced grandkids for them, so I'm pretty much irrelevant."

"I doubt that," Roz said. "They should be proud of you."

He almost spit out his drink. "*You're* saying that? The queen of traditional journalism? I'm the sleazy tabloid guy, remember? Not to mention what came before."

She shrugged. "You're really good at what you do. Maybe our methods aren't the same, but you and *The Beacon* always have me worried."

He was a little bit sorry and a little bit delighted. "The feeling has been mutual," he admitted.

"Really? Oh, good. It sucks to go through panic attacks alone."

"Do you have panic attacks?" he asked.

She looked uncomfortable. "Maybe once every six months. A good reminder of mortality."

"You're getting plenty of reminders this week."

"Getting shot at is almost an improvement over a panic attack," she said, her humor almost hiding her disquiet. She grabbed the bill as the server dropped it on the table and stuck a credit card inside the folder.

"Hey, I'm getting lunch," Alden said.

"Absolutely not. I already don't know how I'm going to repay you for the resort."

"There's no reason to. It's *my* weekend getaway," he said with a smile. "But I'm glad to have you along."

Roz shook her head. "I think that page has already gone to print, and it says you got me the cottage to save my life."

"It's a life worth saving." The server brought back the folder, and Alden resigned himself to watching Roz sign the check. "Aren't you having fun?"

Roz busied herself with putting away her card, then lifted her head, regarded him seriously for a few moments—and smiled.

*Whoa,* that smile—smart and sexy and sunny and intimate, and Alden wanted to kiss it right off her face. But she was already getting up, slinging her bag over her shoulder, and he had to follow.

They put the top up on the convertible to give them a little cover and drove over the causeway to the mainland—the city of Bohemia—in search of Seguro Trucking. As Alden drove,

Roz unpinned her windblown hairdo and brushed out her hair. It was all he could do not to touch it.

When they found the place, he had to admit that Roz had been right—tourists would be really obvious around here. The company was based in a beige warehouse with an office and multiple bays, each closed door big enough to accommodate a box truck. It sat in a commercial park, not far from Bohemia's airport. A few trucks were parked in the lot, all gray with no obvious labels, not even the name of the company.

Alden did one spin through the commercial park, then parked across the street from Seguro at a small strip mall that held multiple businesses, including a butcher, a hydroponics store and a pottery studio. There were enough cars to make his red one a little less conspicuous, but he wasn't entirely comfortable with their parking space on the street side of the lot, facing the industrial park and the trucking company. The view was good, but they could be seen, too.

"Maybe we should have brought your dull little car," he said.

"Hey!" Roz protested. "It's not dull. It's like a space shuttle inside!"

Alden laughed, rolled down the windows and turned off the car. "Let's just say it would be less likely to be noticed."

"Yeah, but we're over here, half-hidden by the hedge, and over there—it looks dead."

She was right. After fifteen minutes, there had been zero activity. After fifteen more, he was bored out of his mind.

"I would suck at law enforcement," Alden said.

"For many reasons," she agreed. At his annoyed look, she added, "But charming ones."

"Are you charmed, Ms. Melander?" he asked, reaching over

to take her hand. He rubbed her knuckles lightly with his thumb.

"You have—charms."

He loved it when she fought her own instincts.

And then she yawned.

"Oh, I get it. I'm boring you," he said, withdrawing his hand.

"No, not at all, it's just that even though I thought I got a lot of sleep, I just haven't worked out all the fatigue from the past few days. I'm dreaming of that bed at Lunaria Lodge."

"So am I."

She laughed at his inflection. "I mean, what a fantastic nap it would make."

"If we were in that bed right now, we wouldn't be napping," Alden said in a low voice, looking her in the eye.

Roz swallowed and didn't say anything, but she licked her lips, once. Blast his timing.

"We can continue this farce, or we can go back to the resort," he said after a minute. "What's your pleasure?"

"My pleasure—" She savored the words, then spoke more briskly. "OK, hanging out at the beach would be a lot better than this, but we're here. It's probably thirty, forty minutes back, with traffic. I say we wait it out, give this a chance. Maybe coming in the afternoon was a bad idea. Once it gets dark, if they're doing anything they shouldn't, they might get more active."

"Nocturnal creatures," Alden joked. "I bow to your sense of duty. Why don't you take a nap? I'll watch. I'll read a book on my phone. If you feel like it later, you can watch, and I'll take a nap."

"You're swell," she said with a smile. Without further ado, she reclined her seat and, within a minute, slipped into the steady breathing of sleep. He watched her, taking in how innocent she looked, how soft, not the ambitious, driving reporter who always gave him a run for his money. But she was that, too, and he realized he found both sides of her equally attractive. He had to remind himself he wasn't in a bed or a beachy cottage. He was in an ugly parking lot in a small car surrounded by industrial buildings. He willed his naughty thoughts to subside and turned to the reading app on his phone, calling up a nonfiction book about modern warfare that immediately killed his wayward thoughts. His life could be a lot worse, he thought. And, as he glanced at Roz, he considered the idea that it could be a lot better.

Though practically, really, how would it ever work between them? She was the lead reporter and editor of the *Courier*. He was the go-getter at *The Beacon*. He'd heard of newspaper marriages in which the spouses worked at rival papers, but in those cases, the publications were a lot bigger, and it was easy to avoid a head-on collision if one reporter worked in, say, sports and another wrote editorials. In that atmosphere, they'd never have a serious conflict of interest.

But in Comet Cove, Alden and Roz were practically tripping over each other. He had a crusty editor and a demanding publisher, and even though *The Beacon* went more for frippery than hard news, it still wanted to be first. Roz was trying to save the *Courier*, or at least save it to sell it, and that meant she could give no quarter. There was no way they could be together for real, not if things continued as they were.

Eventually, though, things would change, and not for the better. It didn't seem likely the *Courier* would make it. He knew the circulation numbers. He knew how well-heeled his publisher was. If it failed—well, Roz wouldn't be competing with him anymore, but from what she'd told him, her mother's finances would be in trouble. Roz might have to be a full-time caretaker. Or she'd find a way for her mom to survive without her—or worse, her mom's declining health would lead to the inevitable—and either way, Roz would go back to her big-city career and leave Florida behind.

Hopelessly distracted from his book, Alden looked over at her again.

Hopeless. Yes, that was the word. The very idea was hopeless. And she was hopelessly beautiful, inside and out. And one could very easily fall hopelessly—

"Oh, hell," he muttered.

True to form, he'd had even less sleep than she had. He put away the phone, rolled up the windows, slouched in his seat and let his own hopeless fatigue, a weariness of bones and soul, drag him under.

# twenty-five

THE SOUND PENETRATED Roz's unsettled dream in the form of gunshots. No, a woodpecker. No—

She opened her eyes. *The stakeout.* She felt overwarm, and it was dark in the car except for the beam of light shining into the driver's-side window. Someone out there was tapping on the glass.

Alden rolled it down. "May I help you, officer?" From the looks of him, he'd just awakened, too. So much for keeping watch.

"May I see your license and registration?" asked the officer, a young, pale woman with tattoos and a take-no-crap attitude. A Bohemia deputy, according to the patch on her sleeve. She probably knew Duke, but Roz didn't want to pull that card.

Alden extracted his wallet from his pocket and handed over the paperwork while Roz looked out the windshield and over the short hedge at Seguro Trucking. Three trucks in its lot were all lit up, lined up at a private gas pump. She gasped, touched the lever on her seat and zoomed from reclining to sitting straight up, overcome with excitement. She caught

Alden scowling at her as the cop shuffled through the documents.

Roz glanced in the side mirror. Oh, boy. Two cop cars blocked them in, blue lights flashing, lighting up the otherwise empty lot. *What do they think, we're Bonnie and Clyde?*

"Have you all been drinking tonight?" the officer asked.

"No, ma'am," Alden replied. Which was true. He'd had a beer at lunch, what, eight hours ago?

"Me either," Roz added when the cop looked her way.

The officer glanced around the tiny car, then contemplated them both. "Wait here. Stay in the car." She disappeared for a few minutes as Roz stared anxiously at Seguro's trucks.

"The trucks aren't moving," Alden whispered, as if they might be overheard.

As ridiculous as that thought was, Roz whispered back. "Maybe because the cops are here?"

"Interesting thought."

The officer reappeared at Alden's window. "What are you two doing here?"

"We're staying over at the resort on Comet Cove," he said. "We were enjoying Bohemia today and got lost, and we were so tired, we thought we'd take a nap. I guess we overslept."

The cop looked as if, one, she didn't buy a word of it, but two, didn't see any real reason to complicate her evening by arresting a couple whose only obvious crime was sleeping in a really weird place.

"You can't stay here," she said, handing him his IDs. "Do you need directions?"

"Uh, no, I'll see if I can get the GPS on my phone working," Alden said. "I'm hopeless with technology."

Roz tried not to laugh as the cop frowned. "I'll help him," she said. "He wouldn't let me help earlier."

The cop grunted. "Typical male. We'll escort you out of the neighborhood."

"I've got this, ma'am," Roz said, holding up her phone, the map already queued to Comet Cove. "Let's go, honey," she said to Alden.

He shot her a sideways glance. "Right, *sweetheart.*"

The cop looked from one to the other and shook her head. As she walked away, Roz heard her mutter, "Dumbass tourists."

The two cop cars backed up, waiting for Alden to leave.

He backed up, too.

*"Alden!"*

He jumped and hit the brakes. "What?"

"You said you were going to keep watch!"

"Nothing was happening." He checked his mirrors and headed forward out of the lot.

"It's happening now," Roz said, looking back at the Seguro trucks as he drove, "and we have to leave!"

"We'll come back," he said confidently.

"Turn right here."

"We are *not* going back to Comet Cove."

"No," she said, "but we want them to think we are. By the way, how did you convince them you're a tourist? Your address is Comet Cove!"

"I haven't changed my license yet. It still says I live in South Florida."

"What are you doing?"

Alden turned in to the parking lot of a fast-food restaurant. "I'm hungry. It's almost eight o'clock."

"But we have to go back!"

"Chill," he said, pulling into the drive-through. "Let's give the police a chance to get out of there, and then we'll go back. We're not going to miss anything."

"How can you know that?"

Alden turned and grinned at her, ignoring her question. "What do you want, *honey?*"

Roz rolled her eyes. "Cheeseburger meal, with a Coke."

He ordered the same thing for both of them and rolled to the next window. This time, she let him pay.

"I'm still mad at you," she said when he grabbed the bag and cups at the next window and handed them to her.

"Eat something and you'll feel better." He reached into the bag and stole a fry.

"You're impossible. What are you doing now?"

"Parking. I have to pee. You?"

Roz had to admit that she did, especially since he suggested it. They hastened inside the restaurant, did their business and ran out.

"I'm heading back to the warehouse," Alden said once they were in the car and munching on their burgers. He drove out of the parking lot. "I'm going to go through the industrial park instead of going back to that lot. Look for our friends with the flashing lights."

They reached the entrance to the industrial park without further interference, demolishing their dinner on the way. Alden turned in, creeping slowly through a maze of roads between nondescript metal buildings, looking for their quarry.

"This is the corner," Roz said, looking at her map app. "Hold up."

They paused at the stop sign and looked down the street in the direction of the warehouse.

"I don't see any cops," Alden said.

Roz frantically scanned the area. "I don't see any trucks, either!"

Alden made a hard turn and accelerated toward Seguro

Trucking, no longer skulking. "We'll catch them. One of them." This time he didn't sound so sure.

"Keep going!" she called when he slowed down near the warehouse. "There's only one other way out of here."

"Wouldn't we have seen them?" he asked.

"Not if they didn't go past the restaurant. Not if they took the other exit. Turn left at the stop sign. Hurry, Alden," she said, unable to keep the anxiety out of her voice.

"Just keep your eyes peeled. It's a truck. It's probably heading for a main road."

He glanced at the digital map on her phone, then navigated quickly from one stop to the next as Roz strained to see in the dark.

"Stupid trucks have no signs on them," she muttered as they got into more traffic. "How are we going to pick it out?"

"The ones that were ready to go had cooling units on the top. Look for that."

"That's weird," she said. "Do drugs need to be kept cool?"

"They could be there to throw people off. Or maybe they're shipping ice cream."

"That would be nice."

"You'd like that, ice cream with your cop friend, wouldn't you?" he asked.

Roz laughed. "You can't possibly be jealous of Duke."

"At least he's convenient," Alden said in clipped tones. "He's not always trying to scoop you on a story."

"Are you?" she asked, taken aback.

"No, my dear, or why would I be driving you on the wild goose chase du jour?"

Roz caught sight of a truck. "There's one!"

Alden flinched at her shout. "Easy, girl. Where?"

She pointed, and he turned.

"That might be one of them," he said. As they got closer, he sounded more interested. "I recognize that sticker."

"You saw a sticker in the dark?"

"I saw it earlier on one of the parked trucks. See it?"

Roz saw it. It was small, a black-and-white decal that showed a hand holding a gun with the words "BACK OFF!"

"That's comforting," she said dryly.

"Look where it's going," Alden mused after a few minutes of weaving through downtown Bohemia. "Over the causeway to the barrier island."

"To Bohemia Beach?"

But a few minutes later, after they'd reached the barrier island, the truck turned south on the beach highway.

"I think it's going to Comet Cove," Alden said, following it onto A1A.

"Maybe." Now Roz was really interested. "Don't lose it."

"I won't lose him now unless he transforms into a boat and shoots off into the water."

She shot him a wry look. "And don't let him see you."

"That's a little harder," Alden said, but he backed off as the truck drove south into more sparsely populated south Bohemia Beach, then into Comet Cove.

"Maybe he's just delivering supplies to a local restaurant or the resort or the Meteor Mart."

"A little late for deliveries."

"You're right," she said, a bit giddy. "They could be here for *anything*. I'm starting to get kind of excited."

"Hold that thought, sweetheart," Alden said, shooting her a smile as he crested the bridge over the inlet, following the mysterious truck.

chapter
# **twenty-six**

ALDEN ENJOYED CALLING ROZ "SWEETHEART." Let her think it was a joke, a flashback to older times, to an old newspaper movie he loved. Anyway, it was better to flirt than to admit he'd screwed up by falling asleep for so long.

He allowed more distance between them and the truck as it trundled south on A1A, then turned west. There really weren't that many places to go here on Comet Cove, and the truck rolled between a few businesses before entering a residential area. After a couple of blocks, it turned left. Alden kept going straight.

"Alden, it's turning!" Roz almost shouted.

"I know. I don't want him to know we're following him. He might be testing us. There aren't any other cars on this road."

"But we might lose it."

"He's clearly trending south and west. I don't think we'll lose it." *Don't lose it,* he told himself. He sped up, then stopped at the next stop sign. "Look left. Tell me if you see him."

They waited for a minute. "I see him, looks like three blocks over. He's going west."

"Good." Alden waited a minute, then turned left, went two blocks and turned right. "We'll parallel him. Keep your eyes peeled in case he doubles back."

They didn't see the truck for a few blocks, despite Alden ignoring speed limits. Finally, they saw it just ahead of them, still one block over, still heading west. They were getting into the Saturn Shores neighborhood, where the roads curved around wiggles in the shoreline, meandering past bigger lots with palatial homes.

"Where's he going?" Roz asked.

"We're running out of road. The lagoon's just ahead."

"So Southside Wharf, maybe."

"Maybe. I'm going to move back east by a block or two," Alden said. "If the marina is where he's going, he'll have to switch, too."

"Hold up at the stop sign," Roz said as he covered the short distance back to the bigger road that led to the wharf. They sat at the intersection and waited and watched. In a couple of minutes, a few blocks south of them, the truck appeared, turning south to head toward the harbor.

"Bingo."

"It's going to meet a boat!" Roz said excitedly as Alden turned in that direction.

"Maybe." Alden found himself more nervous than he cared to admit. If these were drug dealers, they wouldn't take kindly to being watched by a couple of journalists. Or anyone, for that matter. "If it's clear it's going to the wharf, I'm going to park on the street a block away so we're not so obvious."

"Good idea."

The truck headed into the marina, and Alden drove south, then west again, and found a parking space on a tree-lined street. Roz grabbed her phone but left her bag in the car, and they walked toward the marina, entering the parking lot on the south side.

"Where is it?" Roz whispered after they paused behind the tiny sundries store, peering at the poorly lit docks.

Alden considered their options. "There are a couple slips down at the end that bigger boats use for loading. The truck probably went down the marina road."

"Let's go," Roz said.

"Carefully," agreed Alden. "Let's get over to the trees that border the parking lot and walk from there. It's darker, and we can still see the truck."

They slipped into the grassy area under the palms and live oaks. Cautiously, they made their way deeper into the bushes and shadows, paralleling the parking lot and the narrow road that wended through the marina.

He soon spotted the truck. It was backed up to where a boat was docked, probably commercial, maybe for fishing. Or maybe it was just made to look like a fishing boat. A couple of guys were opening the truck's back door.

"That makes some sense," Alden said quietly as they paused behind a dense cluster of bamboo.

"What?"

"The boat looks just as nondescript as the truck, so it's probably not from Consummate Catch," he said, "which we might expect, since we saw one of these trucks actually delivering stuff *to* Consummate's truck."

"But Consummate could be delivering the goods by sea, too," Roz said.

"I don't think so. Look."

A handful of rough-looking guys had appeared on the deck of the boat, carrying a large box out of the hold.

"What *is* that?" Roz exclaimed.

Alden grabbed her by the arm as one of the guys looked in their direction, and they ducked lower into the darkness. After a moment, the curious boatman went back to helping his mates carry the box into the truck.

"Sorry," Roz whispered.

Alden couldn't help himself. He kissed her cheek and put an arm around her. He really didn't want her getting killed.

Roz held up her phone and snapped a couple of photos of the boat, then took a short video while Alden, worried about being seen, wished she'd hurry up.

She finally stopped and stowed her phone in a pocket. "Are they speaking Spanish?" she asked as the men moved more boxes from the boat to the truck.

"I think so. Not really a surprise in Florida. You thinking something more nefarious?"

"You always hear about drug dealers from Central and South America. Just a thought."

"I don't know what to think," Alden admitted. "This could all be completely innocent."

"Except they're doing it all in the dark, in unmarked trucks and unmarked boats."

"So they suck at marketing," he said.

Roz clapped a hand over her mouth and made snuffling noises as she smothered a laugh. Alden felt like laughing, too, only there was that whole thing about not getting killed.

"They're closing up the truck," she whispered.

The boat was already revving up and heading out into the lagoon. From there, who knew? Up the lagoon to Bohemia Harbor? Or through the inlet to the Atlantic and beyond?

"I guess the show's over," Alden said.

"Wait." She grabbed his arm.

The two guys from the truck stood by their vehicle on the marina road, looking into the night. Toward them.

Alden bit back a curse. Instead, he stayed still and silent, holding Roz, willing her to be still, too.

One of the guys pulled a handgun out of his waistband and walked toward them.

Roz pinched Alden's arm, and he could barely keep from crying out. He glared at her. She pointed frantically toward the dark park on the other side of the trees. That might be their only option for escape, but a road lay between this shrubbery and the woodsy park. More to the point, a streetlight lit up that road, guaranteeing they'd be seen.

The first gunman was getting closer. The second guy had produced a nasty-looking shotgun from the cab of the truck and now walked the docks, looking around, moving in their general direction.

Alden dearly hoped the trees and bushes would provide enough cover as they crouched and scampered quickly and quietly away from the marina road and deeper into the landscaping. The park across the street offered a tempting escape. If they could get across the road and its aggravating light, they could disappear into the wild scrub on the other side.

Roz froze, and he bumped into her. Her eyes were wide. He looked over his shoulder. The man with the handgun was no more than ten yards away, peering into the darkness, almost looking right at them.

A raucous cry broke the night as a shape crashed out of the underbrush behind the gunman. He whirled and fired in the direction of the noise, away from the reporters. Alden yanked on Roz's arm, and they sprinted across the street and into the shadows as the cacophony continued. Alden pulled Roz down into the foliage in the well of darkness on the other side of the road and looked back, breathless. A great blue heron flapped wildly around the dock, screeching, and the other trucker—the one with the rifle—yelled at the first guy, gesturing emphatically toward the truck.

The first gunman took one last look around. Then, in apparent disgust, he took one more heedless shot at the poor heron, which shrieked its displeasure and flew off. The shooter trotted back to the truck to join his buddy. In moments, the vehicle rolled out of the marina and back north.

"Eff me, that was close," Alden said, sitting hard on the leaf-covered ground after the truck was out of sight.

Roz panted as she dropped down next to him. "And we didn't find out a darn thing."

"We found out that a truck that is somehow connected with a company that has a connection with Consummate Catch picked up unknown cargo from an unknown boat."

"Well, that," Roz said, "but that's still not front-page material."

He laughed. "You mean you want to actually write a story about this three-ring circus?"

"Eventually, yeah."

Alden found this adorable. He found *her* adorable.

He put an arm around her and kissed her, a light, tantalizing kiss that made him want so much more. But with rocks and branches under his behind, he was uncomfortable and not a little freaked out, and she was actually shivering. He brushed a strand of her escaped hair back behind one ear, and she granted him a small, tremulous smile.

"Let's go home," she said.

Home. *A consummation devoutly to be wished,* he thought,

though Shakespeare was talking about something else entirely, a place they were a hair's breadth away from tonight when they faced down that gun. He wasn't ready to travel into that undiscovered country just yet.

But home with Roz? That would be just fine.

chapter
# **twenty-seven**

WHEN ROZ GOT out of the shower wrapped in one of those fluffy Lunaria Lodge robes, Alden was slouching on the couch. With his ruffled wet hair, in a matching robe, he seemed especially handsome in the warm glow of the pretty paper-shaded lamp on the end table. He looked completely at ease, tapping on his phone, his feet perched on the coffee table. His soles sported scratches from their hike through the swamp. Funny she hadn't noticed how big his feet were before—just one more detail she hadn't had the time to take in. She barely knew him, and yet, she'd fallen into his hands like a baseball in a glove, snug, as if she knew she fit there.

Though, she mused, she was certainly far from his first catch, given his looks. Plus there was the charm, charm she wasn't quite sure she could trust.

And then he glanced up from his phone, and his face broke into a wide, warm smile that made his gray eyes sparkle, and Roz allowed herself to forget her reservations.

Alden put down his phone and poured her a glass of deep red wine from the bottle on the coffee table, then topped off his. She sat next to him and took the proffered glass, savoring the first sip. Definitely a higher quality than she was used to buying.

"What is this?" she asked as he sipped his own.

"One of my favorite cabernets. You like?"

"Mmm." She leaned back against the soft couch and closed her eyes. "So what were those guys doing in the harbor tonight?"

He chuckled. "You're always working, aren't you?"

"In this case, working means trying to figure out who's trying to kill me, so yeah, it's kind of a priority."

"You're safe here," he said.

"You sound so sure."

"I'm sure. Some kind of super manager stopped me when I tried to ask questions around the resort earlier. If anything dangerous is in the offing, I feel confident the security staff will nip it in the bud."

"Super manager, huh?"

"Everything but the cape," Alden declared.

"I feel so much better," Roz said, unable to help her sarcasm.

"You should." He set down his glass, eased closer to her and slipped an arm around her. "You OK?"

"I am now. Once I can lose myself in a hot shower, I always feel better."

He leaned closer, so close she felt his breath on her neck, then whispered in her ear. "Are you sure you want to work?"

"Of course I'm sure!" *No, of course I'm not sure.*

Alden laughed, pulled away and picked up his wine for a sip.

"So we don't know what that boat was unloading," she pressed, "and we don't know where the other two trucks were going, either, because we lost them."

"We couldn't follow three at one time anyway," Alden noted. "Maybe they were also picking up a load of whatever it is."

"Where?"

He shrugged. "Bohemia Harbor? Port Canaveral? Or maybe it was something land-based. They might mix it up to avoid detection."

"We're getting nowhere, aren't we?" Roz couldn't hide her frustration.

"Relax. Drink more wine. This place is made for relaxation." He slouched again, took another sip and let out a sigh of pleasure. "Think they'd let me move in here?"

Roz snorted. "Go ahead. It's the perfect place to research your gossip stories."

"It wouldn't be the same without you."

She stilled, abruptly feeling awkward. She sat up and took a sip of wine.

"What is it, Roz?" Alden asked. He paused, waiting in vain for an answer. "Are you upset?"

"Don't joke about stuff like that," she said.

"I meant it."

"This is—this is what it is. We can't be together. You're *Beacon*. I'm *Courier*."

"Not forever," he said. "Things change."

"Not for the better for me, I think." She drank more wine. It was easier than thinking.

"Don't you feel this?" Alden asked. "I lose my mind around you. Clearly, or I wouldn't be running all over the county getting shot at with you."

"That's flattering," she said wryly.

"It should be." Now he sounded annoyed. "I can't explain

how I feel about you, but it's powerful. Deny that you feel it, too."

Roz didn't say anything. She couldn't deny it. But it was impossible. *He* was impossible. How could he even vocalize it, this idea that they could ever be together?

"When the story is over, this is over," she said. "How can it not be?"

A corner of his mouth turned up. "I don't know. You're clever. Figure it out."

"I can't even figure out why a movie star blew up in the Atlantic Ocean."

"Fuel leak, obviously."

She snickered. "Maybe I'll write that tomorrow and be done with it."

"About tomorrow—"

"Yeah?"

Alden looked at her with a funny expression and shook his head. "Never mind. Want to go to bed?"

"You mean to sleep?"

His response was gentle, but she thought she detected a hint of hurt in his cool tone, and it almost slayed her.

"Whatever you want, Roz," he said.

Brunch at Sirenia wasn't a bad way to start the day. Or at least, that was what Alden thought when he and Roz sat on the deck and ordered fresh-squeezed orange juice and coffee while admiring the sparkling sea view and a wide, golden beach studded with two dozen plastic pink flamingos.

It went downhill from there.

"Boy, you got the scoop today," their industrious server

Lily told Alden. She dropped off their beverages as a healthy Sunday morning brunch crowd, including a cluster of hungover groomsmen, buzzed around them. "What can I get you?"

Alden shot a glance at Roz, whose relaxed expression had just morphed into something between puzzlement and panic.

"Uh, I'll have the Italian omelet with toast," Alden said. "Roz?"

"The grouper Benedict," she said, but Roz wasn't looking at Lily. She was looking at Alden.

"Sure thing!" Lily said. "I'll get that right in for you."

When she left, Roz pulled her phone out of her bag and tapped furiously. Her eyes grew wide.

"You got an interview with Mysty Wellington."

"Well," Alden said uncomfortably, "Kat did."

"But this was your story."

"Yeah, but she's nicer than I am, and celebrities will talk to her more than they'll talk to me. I'm the guy who digs up the dirt behind the scenes, so I'm not very popular."

Roz shook her head and scrolled through the story on the phone. "Mysty is pregnant with Boyd's baby? That's what they were going to celebrate on the carriage ride?"

"That's why he never changed his will. Even after they split, he wanted to leave everything to her and, therefore, his kid. He was going to have a role in the parenting along with Mysty and her future wife. Of course, he didn't know he'd die so soon."

"You scooped me," Roz said in disbelief.

"I almost told you last night. But you did say you didn't care about the gossip story, didn't you?"

She had a dazed look. "What have I been thinking?"

"We're still trying to crack the explosion story. I wouldn't dream of writing anything about that without talking to you first."

"No one is going to give a scrambled egg about the explosion story, if we—if I ever crack it."

Alden didn't like the way "we" became "I."

"Roz," he said, "Kat got this."

"With your help."

"And you don't write gossip," he continued. "You can't hold this against me."

She sipped her coffee and looked out at the sea, where a sailboat cut its way through the deep blue water, its white sail glowing in the morning sun. "Of course I can't hold it against you. I'm a professional, and we work for rival papers, and you need to do your job, and I need to do mine."

Oh, man. She was all frost now. He had thought about telling her. Maybe he should have. She would have let him have his scoop. She was that kind of person. Honorable.

*Crap.*

Roz was tapping on her phone again.

"What are you doing?" he asked.

"Telling Bruce to get an item online about what Mysty told you about the baby. And attributing it to *The Beacon,* of course." The way she said *Beacon,* it sounded as if the word was wrapped in barbed wire.

"Told Kat, not me."

"I wonder if we—I should rule out Mysty having something to do with Boyd's death. She admits she knew she was getting his fortune, after all. That's a strong motive. That's not *gossip.* That could be murder." It was almost like she was talking to herself as she tapped her phone.

"Please don't be mad," Alden said.

Roz stopped her rumination and looked up at him. "Stunned is more like it."

Then their food arrived. With the plates and Lily came Chef Sofia, clad in black and looking unhappy.

"Mr. Knox, I'm pleased to see you here again as a customer," Sofia said in her Italian accent, which sounded a lot more sharp this morning. "But if you ever talk to one of my staff again as a reporter without talking to me first, you will be banned from this property forever. Do I make myself clear?"

Alden opened his mouth to speak, but no sound came out.

"The only reason I'm willing to be civil to you going forward," the chef continued, "is that you helped me sell that ridiculous cupcake." She turned to his brunch mate. "Roz, it's always lovely to see you. Buona giornata."

Chef Sofia stalked off. Lily shot them an embarrassed smile and followed her.

"What did you *do?*" Roz asked.

"I chatted up one of the staff about the seven-hundred-dollar cupcake Boyd had ordered for the carriage ride. I might have, uh, not been entirely clear that I worked for *The Beacon.*"

"What did you tell him?"

"I might have told him I was planning to propose to my girlfriend and needed to plan a carriage ride. But I didn't get that much from the kid!" he protested. "Most of it I put together myself."

"Oh, Alden," Roz said. Her disappointed tone was a knife to the heart.

"It was harmless." OK, maybe he'd been sneaky. But he was just doing his job. And very well, too. "You don't have to be so judgy." He dug into his omelet and chewed, grumpy. Though it was *really* good.

"I'm not judgy," Roz said, taking a bite of her dish. Her face softened slightly as she savored it, and he wanted to scream and grab her by the shoulders and kiss her.

Instead, they ate in silence until Lily came back to check on them.

"This grouper Benedict is absolutely fabulous," Roz said to her.

"Of course, the chef is a genius, but it helps that we get such nice fish. In fact," Lily said, *sotto voce,* "that's our supplier there on the other end of the terrace, having brunch."

Alden and Roz both looked. Two middle-aged couples, tan and attractive in their beachy pastels, laughed over mimosas.

"Who?" Alden asked.

"The man in the pink shirt," Lily said softly. "Peter Verret."

# twenty-eight

"OK, you all let me know if you need anything," Lily added as Alden and Roz gaped at Peter Verret and his friends having brunch, not a care in the world.

The server sped off, and Alden, stunned, locked eyes with Roz.

"No way," she murmured.

"He has a home here, right? One of them?"

"In Comet Cove? Yes, in the Saturn Shores neighborhood."

Alden stole another look at him. "Should we talk to him?"

"What's the point?" she asked. "I don't think annoying him over his brunch is going to do any real good. He's already made his statement, and we have nothing new to ask."

"We could ask him what he transports in his trucks."

She swallowed a bite of her breakfast and shrugged. "Go ahead, if you want to. I prefer to know more before I blunder in and ask uninformed questions."

"You were OK with blundering into his parking lot and spying on Consummate Catch's nighttime operations."

Roz scowled at him. "I wasn't alone, drunken sailor."

"No, you weren't." Alden needed to get this conversation

back on course. "And you aren't alone now. Let's do some more research. Maybe there are connections with Garza other than the trucking operation. And then we'll be able to ask better questions."

She sipped her coffee and looked out at the water, ignoring him. Finally, she turned to face him. Her hazel eyes were tinged with pain, but her voice was calm.

"We'll see this story through, and then that's it."

Alden's heart crumpled like a discarded first draft, and then he was angry at himself for caring so much. It wasn't like anything would have worked out with her.

"Let's go back to the cottage and see what we can find out," he said quietly. "I booked it for one more night."

"I'll be going home tonight," Roz said, "but it's OK if we work there."

Alden nodded, not trusting himself to speak. When did he become so vulnerable, so wrapped up in her? It had happened so fast, hit him so hard, that he couldn't imagine it was over.

They walked back to the villa in silence. The air was fresh with salt and flowers. The birds sang. It should have been romantic. Damn it, it *was* romantic. But Roz, who wore a pretty green skirt and flowing white blouse and sandals that made her all too irresistible, had built an invisible wall around her that he didn't dare assail.

"Why don't we use your laptop?" Alden suggested when they got back inside. One computer, he thought, meant they'd have to sit together.

Roz didn't object, and he sat next to her on the couch, where they'd been so cozy the night before. Even if she'd chosen sleep over shenanigans.

Slowly, as they searched the Internet and reviewed everything they knew about Verret's fishing business and Garza's trucking business, her chilly attitude seemed to thaw, until he almost felt they were back to where they'd been.

Except that she was going home tonight. And she was still in danger.

"So Verret and Garza serve on the board of this ocean awareness charity together," Roz said.

"And they promote sport fishing, clean beaches and oceans, that sort of thing, right?" Alden asked.

"Right."

"See who else is on the board."

Roz scrolled through the names, and they started running searches on each of them against Verret and Garza.

"Check this out!" she said. "This guy Louis Smythe is on the nonprofit board with them, and he's also on that state task force that's going after illegal offshore fishing, the one that Verret is a consultant for."

"So check him out," Alden said.

It didn't take them long to find old stories that said Smythe once served on a drug task force that had been investigated for corruption. He had never been charged.

"Drugs again," Roz said.

"It's not enough, though, is it?" Alden mused, sitting back.

"Something's missing." She fell back against the cushions, too, tapping her lips as she thought, a nervous habit that drew Alden's attention to her mouth. Gawd, he was a mess.

"Why don't we take a walk on the beach and talk it out?" he suggested.

Roz shot him a look that he couldn't read. "I guess it couldn't hurt," she said. "We might as well enjoy this place while we've got it."

*And enjoy each other,* he wanted to add.

They left their shoes in the cottage and took the sandy

track between the dunes, lined with swaying sea oats and sea grapes. It led down to an empty beach.

It was just after low tide, he thought. Thousands of small shells created swaths of twinkling color on the sand as the waves washed over them and retreated with a soft hiss.

He and Roz stepped past the shells and let the water swirl around their feet. Late on this warm afternoon, the ocean was calm. The scene entranced him. Way out on the tip of the point, the lighthouse's red-and-white stripes gleamed in the sunlight. The lighthouse looked hazy at this distance, almost like a toy.

The breeze blew Roz's loose clothes against her body and rippled his white linen shirt. He'd rolled up his khakis, and his feet felt good on the wet sand. He should be able to forget his troubles, but they were right there, all around him.

She was right there.

"Let's sit for a minute," Alden said, gesturing to a lumpy cluster of rocks by the tree line. He wanted her close to him, hoping their physical connection might heal the rift between them.

"OK." Roz sounded hesitant, but she followed him up the beach. They sat on the cool rocks, under the swaying fronds of several palm trees, and looked out over the ocean. The light took on an amber glow as the sun lowered behind them and the magic hour approached.

"Is that a shrimping boat?" Roz asked as a vessel headed out from the inlet.

"I think so."

"I don't think I'll ever look at a fishing boat again without thinking of that one blowing up."

"Only that one wasn't a commercial fishing boat," Alden said.

"I guess nobody's going to stop fishing just because one boat blew up."

"It's a huge business," he agreed.

Roz looked at him strangely. "It's a huge business."

"That's what I said."

"Verret consults with law enforcement to stop illegal fishing."

Alden looked at her. "And Smythe is on that task force. And he and Verret and Garza are all on that nonprofit together."

"Maybe Verret isn't giving information to the task force," she said. "Maybe it's the other way around."

"He's getting information on illegal fishing? No—information on law enforcement," Alden said, catching her line of thought. "So he can avoid the fishing police?"

"He or his cronies. Maybe they're all involved. Somebody catches the fish—they run a private fleet out of Mexico or South Florida or wherever. Garza picks up the illegally caught fish from the boats and delivers them to Consummate Catch to supplement Verret's regular haul."

"Hence the refrigerated trucks," Alden said.

"Verret 'launders' the fish, like dirty drug money. Sells them through his legit operation. Makes a huge profit."

"I read up on illegal fishing in my research," Alden said, feeling a twinge of excitement. "It adds up to billions of dollars' worth of fish each year. A lot of the boats are from Mexico. These guys have no scruples. Their methods kill thousands of fish and turtles that should never be caught—they use illegal long lines, gill nets. It's really destructive."

"So much for 'green' fishing techniques," Roz said. "They could be using anything. Verret's guides know all the good fishing spots. He told me so. Even if the guides aren't involved,

Verret could pass that information on to his fishing fleet, the legal one and the illegal one. Suppose his own bad guys were somehow involved in Boyd Bellamy's death?"

A noise behind them, on the other side of the rocks, caught Alden's ear. He twisted to look, then stood, followed by Roz.

"Just suppose they *were* involved in that overpaid actor's death," said a man in black, pointing a handgun at them as he emerged from the trees. "Something terrible might happen to someone who wanted to know."

Alden knew that rough voice. It was the same man who'd tried to kidnap Roz.

"Froggy," he whispered to Roz.

"Oh, great," she whispered back.

The gun, a Smith & Wesson M&P, he thought, was equipped with a silencer. Not just a scare tactic, then.

"What did you say?" Froggy asked, stepping closer.

"You can't do anything to us." Alden spoke up with an optimism he didn't really hold as he wondered where the bodyguard was. And then he remembered: He'd asked for security only when Roz was alone. Because he had the crazy idea he could protect her himself.

Roz stood next to him and reached for his hand. He squeezed it, wondering if this would be his last chance.

chapter
## twenty-nine

THEY'D BEEN *SO CLOSE*.

Roz had felt the thrill of finally homing in on the truth, about to figure out their mystery, only to be slammed with a surreal rush of fear a moment later.

"You can't do anything to us," Alden had told the wiry gunman—Froggy—and she'd grabbed Alden's hand out of instinct.

"It'll be just another drug killing." Froggy's thin, pale face and dark eyes grew animated. "Or maybe a car accident. Or drowning? A lovers' swim gone awry, after I provide a nice strangulation? I haven't decided yet."

"We're pretty harmless," Roz said, trying not to let his tone get to her. "Why would you want to kill us?"

"You've already stuck your nose way too far into something that's none of your business."

"I'm a journalist," she said, pondering what it would take to distract the man and run away. "Everything is my business. And illegal fishing is the public's business."

"Puh-leeze," Froggy said. "If you'd just written about the fuel leak, everybody would've been happy."

"Boyd Bellamy wasn't happy," she retorted.

"It was a fuel leak?" Alden asked.

Froggy smirked. "Of course it wasn't, but it wasn't really our fault that the boat's anchor got tangled up in one of our nets in just the wrong spot."

"And pulled up an unexploded bomb!" Roz exclaimed, unable to contain her glee. She'd seen the netting in her pictures of the debris but didn't put it together until now.

"You're a morbid little beeyatch, aren't you?" the gunman said. "We came to the same conclusion, since we didn't blow it up. It wasn't their lucky day."

"The bombs made it a perfect fishing spot. Anything on the bottom attracts fish," Alden said, almost to himself.

Roz added it up in her head. The charter boat carrying Boyd Bellamy had fished at one of Consummate Catch's secret fishing spots, which their poachers knew about, too. Where the illegal fishing operation had dropped some kind of net that got entangled with an unexploded bomb dropped sometime after World War II. Crazy!

"We don't have to write anything," Alden was saying to Froggy. "You can let us go."

The man shook his head, then nodded toward Roz. "She'll never agree to that. I can tell just from her face."

Roz tried to make her face a mask, but the sicko was right. She'd come too far on this story to back down. Not only did Peter Verret's operation kill a perfectly innocent man—two men—but they did it to protect a huge illegal fishing operation that could seriously damage future catches, maybe even push some fish to extinction. It seemed like sportsmen, commercial operations and fish connoisseurs alike wouldn't appreciate that outcome. And that seemed like the public's business to her.

Therefore it was her business, her job to report it. If she got out of this alive.

If *they* got out of this alive. She sucked in a breath as Alden released her hand and took a slight step forward. He was trying to protect her, but she didn't want him to. She didn't want him to get hurt. A thousand thoughts went through her head at once, a thousand feelings. He could've been more straightforward about *The Beacon*'s scoop this morning, but they *had* made an agreement. And they were competitors. Maybe she'd overreacted. Worse, she didn't know how to deal with all the feelings she had, and she didn't handle those very well, either. She cared for him. She couldn't let him—

"Let her go," Alden said.

"This is a package deal, lover boy," Froggy said. "But we're not going to do it here. I need you to come out from behind those rocks and step this way."

"I'd rather stay here," Alden said.

"I'm not above shooting you here. I'm equipped for it." He waved the gun at them. "If you want to be shot here, fine. But I'll make another stop. You know where, don't you, Ms. Melander?"

Roz felt a chill. "You wouldn't."

"I know where your mother lives. I know a lot about you, since our guys found your boat."

"What were they doing out there?" Roz asked, dying of curiosity. Perhaps literally.

"Getting the gill net, or what was left of it."

Alden took another step toward Froggy, giving up the negligible cover of the rocks. "How did you know we were here?"

"My boss noticed you at the restaurant this morning after the chef yelled at you. He gave me a heads-up, and I followed you."

Alden looked at Roz and mouthed the word, "Sorry."

She almost laughed. And almost cried.

"Enough delays." Froggy raised his guttural voice. "Are you coming with me, or do I have to do this here? Wouldn't you rather have one last walk with your sweetie?"

Roz wanted to kick the guy for his mocking tone, but all she could think was, *no,* this wasn't her last walk with Alden. It couldn't be.

She moved first, but Alden was already two steps ahead of her. Before she could advance, he reached back and shoved her to the ground, even as he jumped forward.

Thrown to the sand, with the rocks between her and Froggy, Roz heard the shot.

And screamed.

She scrambled to her feet. Alden lay face-down in the sand in front of her, his white shirt spattered with blood.

"No!" she cried, leaping to his side and crouching next to his still body. He couldn't be gone. Not like this. "Alden!"

"Yes?" came Alden's muffled reply. He groaned and rolled over, spitting sand. "I'm fine."

"*What?*" she exclaimed. "The blood!"

"It's not mine."

Alden sat up, and both of them looked around. A grimacing Froggy sprawled in the sand, clutching his thigh, trying to stanch the blood flowing from an apparent gunshot wound. His gun lay several feet away. And beyond him, a neatly dressed, tan man with cropped brown hair emerged from the woods with his own handgun. He looked like he'd just stepped off a golf course.

Roz flinched. "Oh, crap."

The new guy, his muscles barely contained by his yellow

polo shirt, held up a calming hand. "Sorry about the scare, ma'am. I couldn't fire unless I knew you were safe. I was trying not to endanger you. Though *you* didn't help," he said to Alden, who clambered to his feet and pulled Roz up with him.

"I hit the dirt once I realized you were there," Alden said.

*After he'd made sure I was safe,* Roz thought. "And who are you?" she asked their rescuer.

"This is, uh, Kevin." Alden seemed embarrassed. He knew Kevin?

"I'm from Carapace Protection Services," Kevin added. "Mr. Knox here asked us to keep an eye out for you when you were on your own, so I'm afraid I wasn't as close as I should have been, since you weren't. On your own, that is."

"No, she wasn't," Alden said, grabbing her hand again.

"I had an alert from one of the staff that there might be trouble," the bodyguard said.

"Super Manager must've told him," Alden murmured. "Kevin registered with Lunaria's security team. You're not the first guest his firm has guarded here."

"You had someone watching me?" Roz asked Alden.

Alden wore a worried look. "Just to make sure you were OK."

She was kind of annoyed. But as meddlesome as he'd been, Alden had saved her. Almost sacrificed his life for her. Again.

Roz touched his face, looked into his troubled gray eyes and decided not to imagine what could have happened to him. She didn't think she could handle the idea of a world without Alden. Even if she couldn't have him.

"Will one of you hacks call an ambulance?" Froggy grumbled from the ground.

"Watch your mouth," Alden said.

The bodyguard was already tapping his phone.

"And get the police, too," Roz said.

"Duke," Alden said with a frown, and she laughed.

"We'll get rid of him as quickly as we can," she said. "We have a story to write."

chapter
# **thirty**

ROZ KNOCKED AS she entered her mother's house. "Mom?"

"In here," came Megan Melander's voice from the living room. The aide clattered in the kitchen, and the smell of something savory cooking filled the air. Good. She worried about her mom eating enough.

But her mother looked fine today. She got up to hug Roz, and she had a smile on her face. Megan's air of health gave her daughter hope that maybe the disease had slowed, that they would have more good years. Or maybe it was just a good day. She would take whatever blessings she could get.

Major Tom trotted out of the kitchen and jumped up on the coffee table, which was strewn with legal papers.

"Off, Tom," her mother scolded, and the cat leapt to the couch.

Roz knew what those papers were.

"So you made a decision?" Roz asked.

"It's the only one I can make, honey. You know that, don't you?"

"I know." Roz sat next to her on the couch. "I just don't know what comes next."

"None of us do."

That was the truth. It had been two weeks since she and Alden broke the story about the explosion and the illegal fishing operation in a double-bylined article that appeared in both papers. They'd built up to it with a few days of online bulletins, independently written, while together they gathered all the information they needed for the big story. "Together" meaning virtual meetings, emails and phone calls.

Verret's refusal to comment didn't matter so much after he was charged with attempted murder-for-hire, plus negligent homicide for the deaths of Boyd Bellamy and the fishing guide. Subsequent raids on his and Garza's operations resulted in more charges related to the fishing cartel. It seemed the men had been close since the days when Verret got caught with Garza's drugs on board his boat.

Their cohort on the task force had vanished and also was under suspicion, and the Coast Guard was widening the investigation. Forensics on the debris, along with scans of the ocean floor, confirmed that Boyd Bellamy's charter had indeed encountered an unexploded bomb, which became entangled in the poachers' net and was dredged up with the boat's anchor. It was unclear whether the bomb made it all the way to the surface, but the disturbance was enough to blow up the unstable ordnance and the boat. That angle led to more concerns about the safety of boats and beachgoers and a lot of attention for both publications.

The day after the story came out in print, Roz joined Janice at the animal-shelter fundraiser concert at the Moonlight, and for the first time in a long time, a few people actually came up to her and said nice things and asked her questions. Some of it was morbid curiosity about the attempts on her life, of course. And Roz had no illusions about her vocation. There was always someone who wanted to shoot the messenger when the story wasn't something they liked. But in this case, there was cut-and-dried wrongdoing, and the drama didn't hurt. Roz was reminded what it was like to really make an impact with her work.

Then, over wine afterward at The Orbit bar, Roz told Janice maybe a little too much about her feelings concerning a certain handsome reporter.

The whole experience had been exhausting, but the two weeks since the story ran had been thrilling, too. Their pieces were picked up across the state and beyond. While Roz was busy with follow-ups, she was able to stop thinking about Alden for seconds at a time. *Ha!* But she loved the work, and she'd started to wonder what it would mean to keep doing it—maybe even here, in Comet Cove.

And then Mom got the offer to sell the *Courier.*

It would hurt to lose the community chronicle their family had built. They weren't sure yet who the buyers were, as they were acting through a special corporation set up for the sale, but Roz hoped the newspaper would endure. For the town. For the staff.

"I don't know if I want to stay, even if the *Courier* keeps printing," Roz told her mom. "I don't know how much say I'd have anymore. I could go back to the investigative team in Baltimore." Truth was, she'd already sent out feelers and was assured she'd be welcome.

Megan looked down at Major Tom and scratched under his chin. "You know I'll miss you."

The sorrow in her mother's voice cut Roz to the quick. "I'll visit often, I promise. It's just that in the city—I felt like I could really make a difference there," she argued, to herself as much as to her mom. "I had a chance to be someone."

Her mother looked up. "You're already someone extraordinary. And don't you think you've made a difference here? Look at the stories you've written in the past few weeks."

Roz reached out and ran her hand down the cat's back. Her mother knew her better than she thought. "Yes, I think those stories are important. But not all the stories in Comet Cove are that big. I mean, pretty much none of them are."

"Honey, big stories aren't the bread and butter of what we do. They're important, but it's the little stories that really matter. The zoning and council meetings and schools and clubs and even the weddings and the festivals and the fun stuff. Informing the community makes us a stronger community. Besides, isn't our legacy worth something?"

"Of course it is. That's not what I meant." Roz wondered if she'd offended her mother. "What you and Dad did for Comet Cove, it was really important."

"The first draft of history," her mom said, echoing Roz's father.

"You're right. I just don't know if it's that way anymore. Times have changed. Circumstances, too. The new owners might not want me here." And there was *The Beacon*. And the pain of having to face Alden Knox every day.

True to her word, she'd pushed him away after the big piece ran, outside of a few necessary and unemotional emails as requests and reactions poured in. She needed time to think. Yes, she wanted him. Of course she wanted him. But even if the situation wasn't impossible, could she trust him?

For some reason, she'd thought—maybe even fantasized— that he might pursue her after the article ran, despite their differences. It was unreasonable of her, she knew, to expect him to follow her around like a puppy after she'd blown him off, but now it would take a serious gesture to convince her that he had her best interests at heart.

And there had been nothing outside of those few impersonal emails. No calls. No texts. Not even run-ins at the coffee shop.

But this cooling-off period wouldn't last forever. Eventually she'd have to see him, and it wouldn't be cool at all. The encounter would be fevered, agonizing—at least in her heart—even if they didn't say a word. Because Roz couldn't bear the pain of not having him, of having been foiled by her own lousy judgment and, maybe worse, of knowing he didn't want her after all.

The best thing for her was a clean break. She expected to leave the *Courier* in the hands of some media conglomerate—she shuddered at the thought of who that might be—and head back to Baltimore. Roz wanted to take care of her mom, but she also wanted to move on. And staying in Comet Cove was not going to be the best way to do that.

Especially if it meant being haunted by Alden Knox.

chapter
# thirty-one

"ANY PHONE CALLS?" Alden asked John when he got into the office.

"Check your dang voicemail," his editor growled. John tilted back in his desk chair, reading a fresh copy of the *Courier* and snapping his gum. "And you're late."

"I mean, were there calls to the main line, for me."

"If you're expecting a call, wouldn't it come to your personal line?" John asked, shooting Alden a significant look. "Especially a *personal* call?"

"Never mind," Alden said. John was way too perceptive sometimes. "I have an appointment. I'll be back in an hour or so."

He walked outside, got in his car and drove to the parking lot at Comet Cove's cute little boardwalk, which ran along the northeast stretch of the inlet. The boardwalk linked a row of waterfront businesses with the park where Boyd Bellamy had planned to have his picnic. The charming green space, with its pier, playground, bandshell and kid-friendly fountain, was often the site of craft shows, festivals and concerts.

More to the point for Alden, one of the businesses was the Milky Way, which had just opened for the day. It was 11 a.m.

Surrounded by palm trees, the cozy white stucco building was the size of a two-car garage, with a bright blue roof and a small dining area inside. He paused at the patio. Under a blue awning that also shaded the outside service window, a hand-painted menu hung. It touted a couple dozen flavors of ice cream, sundaes and such, along with burgers, hot dogs and baskets of the Milky Way's signature crispy, salty french fries.

There were more tables outside than in, letting guests enjoy the view of the inlet as they ate their treats. But it was early for lunch and a weekday, so Alden was the only customer. He sat alone at one of the square metal tables on the patio that overlooked the water. He waited. He didn't look at his phone. He didn't think about his next story. He just waited.

At eleven twenty, he looked at his watch, stood and sighed. His gaze traveled from the sparkling water before him to the bridge to his west, and he thought about that morning when he and Roz had each come to Star Harbor to try to get the facts on a little story about an exploding boat. He might have written: *That's where our story started.* And then, he thought: *Here is where it ends.*

He had his keys out and was about to get into his Miata in the parking lot when he felt another car slide in next to him. He almost didn't hear it because the smug hybrid made so little noise.

Alden tried not to get his hopes up as he turned to see Roz step out. She had a *Courier* in her hand.

He walked around the front of their cars so he could see all of her. He swallowed. She was pretty—radiant, even. Her chestnut hair was twisted up in a messy bun, her pale green blouse brought out the glint of green in her hazel eyes, and her jeans hugged her tantalizing curves. Casual became her. She was herself. Just the way he liked her.

Roz looked him over. "Sorry I'm late. It took me a while to get to the classifieds this morning."

"You're not late." He hoped it wasn't too late.

"I understand we have a debt to settle."

"I was afraid you wouldn't see the ad. Or you wouldn't come."

"But it was such a tempting offer." She held up the newspaper and read: *"Dear R: IOU forgiven. I'll buy you a cone instead. 11 @ Milky Way. AK."*

"I wanted to be sure you didn't think it was from your buddy Duke."

She laughed. "I already paid my debt to Duke."

"You did?" A spike of jealousy made Alden wince.

"I sent a couple of pints of Ben & Jerry's down to the office for him and Deputy Byrd."

Alden smiled brightly to mask his relief. "Good thinking. Maybe it'll soften her up for next time."

"I doubt it." Roz paused. "Though I don't think I'll have to worry about a next time." She looked unnervingly serious.

"Come on. We'll get a table," Alden said, not mentioning he'd been keeping one warm. "Let me get you something."

"I don't know."

"Please, Roz."

After a moment, she nodded and walked with him to the Milky Way's patio and sat at the same table he had. *That table has a vibe*, he thought. *Maybe this will become our table.*

"Preferences?" Alden asked.

"Butter pecan?"

"Be right back."

Alden returned a few minutes later. "Here's your scoop."

He heard the irony in the word as he handed her a butter pecan cone and sat opposite her with his bowl of mint chocolate chip. They ate in the safety of silence for a minute before he spoke again.

"What did you mean about no next time?" he asked.

"We're selling the *Courier*. Mom's taken care of. There's— no reason for me to stick around."

Was he mistaken, or did she have a question in her eyes, her voice as she said so?

"I know about the *Courier*," he said softly.

"Ha," Roz said, taking a big lick of her cone. "Scooped me again."

"My publisher is buying it."

She stopped licking and stared at him, a stunned look on her face. "So he's going to shut it down?" She sounded heartbroken.

Alden ate a spoonful of his ice cream to fortify himself. "He and I had a long talk about the *Courier*. About its history here. About its fantastic editor. About how well we work together."

She was shaking her head.

He plunged on. "He doesn't want to close it. He wants to combine the staffs and rename the new paper *The Courier-Beacon*. But only if the editor stays on, so it has that imprimatur of the Melander family."

"He what?" Roz stared at him, taking a second to digest what he'd said. "But—the *Courier* covers news."

"So would *The Courier-Beacon*."

"I'm going back to Baltimore. I have a career." This time her protest seemed less vehement, and Alden warmed to his cause.

"Being managing editor of *The Courier-Beacon* would be a

career, too, if on a smaller scale," he said. "It's kind of an honorary title—with a raise, of course—because you'd still be reporting on the biggest stories. You want that, don't you?"

"I wouldn't want to give up reporting," she admitted.

"And you might want to ask yourself if you're out to make a difference or if you're out to make your career. I know something about that, and I think you can make the biggest difference here. For Comet Cove." Alden took a breath. "For me."

Her ice cream dripped onto her hand as she gaped at him. "Rats," she said, looking down.

He set down his bowl and slipped into the chair next to hers.

She looked up at him. "Alden?"

"Say yes. Say you'll stay."

"What will you do?"

"What I've always done. I'll cover society news. I'm good at it, and that's what the publisher wants. But I want to do real news, too—with you. You've given me a taste for it again, and my publisher is starting to understand the power of the free press. That's all thanks to you."

"What about my staff?"

"Anyone who wants to stay can stay. Generous severance if anyone wants to go."

"That's—that's fantastic." Roz's cone was dripping again. Alden took the cone out of her hand and pushed it into his bowl on the table, then took both of her hands in his and gently licked off the stray drips of ice cream. Then he kissed the back of each hand, once. He looked into her eyes, willing her to agree. To see.

"But I had a plan," she said.

"Plans change. This way, the *Courier* lives on. In the name. In you."

"There's that." She searched his eyes. "Did you make this happen?"

He said nothing, but he saw the realization kindle a light in her gaze.

She took a deep breath. "We were thrown together for such a short time. I thought maybe it was just a game for you."

"I don't call being chased, shot at and threatened much of a game."

"Not the story," Roz said—and then, as if it cost her a great deal, "me."

Alden squeezed her hands and moved closer so their knees touched. He felt the spark, and it fueled his declaration. If he didn't tell her everything now, there might never be another chance.

"I'm in love with you, Ms. Melander. I'm in love with your stubbornness and your high standards. I'm in love with your infuriating righteousness. I think I fell in love with you the first time you asked about irrigating golf courses at a zoning meeting. And I want to spend a year writing poems about your hair and your eyes and your mouth."

She raised an eyebrow. "I thought you were going to write a novel."

"That, too. I'm thinking of calling it *Scandal Sheets* by A.A. Knox."

"See, that's just it!" Roz withdrew her hands from his. She stood and paced, tears forming in her eyes. "A.A.? I don't know you nearly well enough, Alden. I've never even asked you your middle name!"

"It's Alden."

"What?"

"My middle name is Alden."

"Then what's your first name?"

He grimaced. "Archibald."

Through her tears, she started laughing.

"Exactly." He held up his hands in a helpless gesture. "This is why I don't tell people my first name. In fact, I think you're the only one, ever." Alden stood, too, walking toward her, slowly backing her up against the wall in the dappled shade of a palm tree. He was inches away from her, but it might have been miles. "You know everything about me that matters. Is it enough? Am *I* enough? You'd get to be the boss of me, you know."

She looked up at him. "You and I are so different, Alden. Archibald."

"Shut up and talk to me."

"You're smart. You're resourceful. You're even a good guy, though you try hard to hide it. And what you've done for my mother—all I can say is thank you," Roz said. "To merge the papers would be so good for everyone. But I don't know if you need me to do it. In fact, I might be more of a hindrance. It's like you and I come from two different planets. How could we ever make this work?"

"Didn't you hear me? I love you, Rosalind Melander. My spaceship has set down on your world. My comet has landed in your cove. Wait, that didn't sound right."

Roz giggled.

He let out an exasperated breath. "I come in peace. Don't you believe me?" And wasn't that enough? God, he hoped it was enough.

"Oh, Alden." She reached up cupped his cheek. And then she slipped her arms around his neck, and time stood still as birds twittered and a sea breeze sighed and a distant boat droned.

"You are extraordinary, and I believe you," Roz said. "And I believe *in* you, you impossible man."

Alden yanked her to him and covered her mouth with his, pouring into her all the love and energy it had taken him to convince his publisher to make the deal, with all the passion that had consumed his soul since Roz walked into and out of his life. She tasted like butter pecan and forever.

He made himself take a breath, to make sure of her. Roz looked up at him, flushed and happy and lovely. Her hair was coming out of the bun, and he wanted to shake it loose, run his hands through it, do things he really shouldn't do on the Comet Cove boardwalk.

"You'll stay?" he asked, burning for her response.

Her smile widened, and her lovely eyes twinkled. "Yes, Alden."

*She said yes.* "And you ... do you feel the same way?"

She gave him a flirty glance from under her eyelashes. "You'll have to do a *lot* more reporting to find out." Then she laid a kiss on him that made his heart soar like a rocket.

When the kiss ended several sultry seconds later, Alden embraced her, and she hugged him back even harder, almost taking his breath away.

"You're squishing me," he told her.

"Do you mind?" She snuggled even closer.

"Not at all. Should we go on a date or something?" he murmured in her ear. "A carriage ride?"

Roz loosened her hold and smiled up at him. "But we're not movie stars."

"Better, sweetheart." Alden grinned. "We're *The Courier-Beacon.*"

# afterword

Thanks for reading! Roz and Alden will return in *Pen and Peril.*

Get notified about the next release in my newsletter. Sign up for fun original content, giveaways, news and cocktail recipes, and I'll send you free stories. I also have a Facebook group where readers can hang out and chat about books and life—please join us in Lucy's Lounge. And you can always find me at LucyLakestone.com!

If you enjoyed this mystery, you might also like my Bohemia Bartenders Mysteries. Mixologist Pepper Revelle joins a team of bartenders who travel to events where life is a cocktail of fun, until it's shaken into madcap mayhem ... and murder.

The Bohemia Bartenders Mysteries are funny whodunits with a dash of romance set in a convivial collective of cocktail lovers, eccentrics and mixologists. These quasi-cozy culinary comedies contain a hint of heat, a splash of cursing and shots of laughter, served over hand-carved ice.

The series starts with *Risky Whiskey.*

## About the book

*Stirring up trouble in New Orleans …*

Eager to shake up her drinks and her life, mixologist Pepper Revelle jumps at an invitation to join the elite Bohemia Bartenders. Leader Neil thinks she'll be the perfect advance gal for his team at a colorful cocktail convention in her hometown of New Orleans, but the job turns out to be more bananas than a drunk monkey. Setting up the key tasting for their distiller client, she and Neil discover their whiskey has gone dangerously bad. But how? And was this shocking poisoning more than an accident?

As Pepper and Neil try to figure out what happened, keep the drinks flowing and help distiller Dash Reynolds survive the weekend, they find themselves the target of increasingly scary attacks. Maybe it's the danger, or maybe it's the drinks, but Pepper also can't help an inconvenient attraction to cocktail nerd Neil as they stir up trouble and try to figure out who's out to get them — before they're sliced and squeezed like a lemon twist in a Sazerac.

All the links: lucylakestone.com/risky-whiskey/

# notes and thanks

I come from a journalism background, and as a rule, reporting isn't nearly as silly and exciting as it gets in *Scoop and Scandal.* That said, I've always loved funny movies about journalists, so in this plot, I've mixed authenticity with a dash of screwball comedy. *His Girl Friday* is my favorite newspaper film. Extra points if you spot the references to the movie and its actors. And regarding authenticity: The "-30-" at the end of the text is the traditional newspaper mark that signified to an editor the end of a story. Its origins are debatable.

This book began as *Desire on Deadline,* a hot novel of romantic suspense in Roxanne St. Claire's Barefoot Bay World. I'm grateful for her invitation to write in her setting. When the rights to the book reverted to me, I was able to lift out my characters and story, transform and enhance them, and plant them in an entirely new place adjacent to my other fictional settings, particularly Bohemia and Bohemia Beach. This book isn't steamy like the first version, but it is unabashedly a romantic mystery. And I anticipate more mysteries starring Roz and Alden in Comet Cove.

Comet Cove is a fictional town, and I've played with the geography of Florida's east coast to create an inlet and a wide stretch of barrier island that will accommodate it. So it's not based on any existing town or inlet, even if Comet Cove is real in my imagination.

In an era when newspapers are struggling or being

purchased by owners with more interest in money and influence than in good old-fashioned journalism, it seems more important than ever to celebrate journalism that aims to report the truth, however unlovable it may be. I respect and honor my many colleagues over the years who have done their job with grit and empathy and dedication to reporting news vital to our everyday lives and happiness, working long hours for little gain. Good journalism keeps the elected officials who are supposed to be working for us accountable. It celebrates everyone from Little League champions to brilliant scientists. It shows us our flaws so we can work on fixing them. It finds the quirky and interesting, the brave and funny, the delicious and daring, and brings them to light, building our sense of community in the process. Freedom of the press is freedom for all of us.

Thank you to Florida Star Fiction Writers, who are a constant source of joy and encouragement. Ample gratitude goes to my perspicacious editor, Holly Martin, who knows her way around a deadline. And thanks to Karen Ann Dell for her valuable feedback on the first version of this book.

Thank you to Mr. Lakestone for making this adventure possible. I owe him a fine bottle of rum.

And thank you, dear reader, for taking a chance on Roz and Alden.

# Books by Lucy Lakestone

**BOHEMIA BARTENDERS MYSTERIES**

These funny mysteries star Pepper Revelle and a team of mixologists who travel to colorful events where life is a cocktail of fun, until it's shaken into madcap mayhem—and murder.

RISKY WHISKEY

BAFFLED BY BITTERS - *story free to subscribers*

WRECKED BY RUM

VEXED BY VODKA

JIGGERED BY GIN

BEGUILED BY BOURBON

SHOCKED BY CHAMPAGNE

WHY OH RYE?

SMOKED BY SCOTCH

BOHEMIA BARTENDERS COCKTAIL COLORING BOOK

**COMET COVE MYSTERIES**

SCOOP AND SCANDAL

PEN AND PERIL

# about the author

Lucy Lakestone writes books that offer fun escapes, whether they're humorous mysteries, hot romances or storm-chasing adventures (as Chris Kridler). She loves sipping a classic cocktail and chasing tornadoes, but not at the same time. An award-winning author and photographer, she's also told stories as a journalist and video producer. She lives on Florida's Space Coast, which inspires many of the colorful settings in her books.

*Learn more at* LucyLakestone.com

facebook.com/lucylakestone

instagram.com/mslucylakestone

amazon.com/Lucy-Lakestone

bookbub.com/authors/lucy-lakestone

goodreads.com/lucylakestone

bsky.app/profile/lucylakestone.bsky.social

pinterest.com/lucylakestone

threads.com/@mslucylakestone

youtube.com/@lucylakestone

www.ingramcontent.com/pod-product-compliance
Lightning Source LLC
Chambersburg PA
CBHW030023200726
48283CB00012B/792